Bug

Bug

Normandy D. Piccolo

NBI
Normandy's Bright Ideas
Florida

Contents

Yesterday was a long time ago.

Fireflies

Light.

Dark.

Light.

Dark.

Light.

Dark.

It is what I saw at night while I lay on my back in the soft, dewy grass and watched the fireflies dance up above in the sky on warm summer nights.

Momma used to say the ones who made the letter *J* were boys who tried to get a girl to like them. But sometimes, she warned, it could be a girl pretending to be a boy to devour her competition.

"Always gotta keep your eye out for that whore tryin' to swoop in and steal your man, Bug," she sternly warned me.

I did not even know what a *whore* was back then. Only someone momma hated. Someone I eventually and unwillingly evolved into. Just like her. Just like those tricky female fireflies.

Fireflies were my escape when I was a young child. I was mesmerized by their soft, enticing glow. It seemed so warm. Safe. Like the comfort one found in the loving arms of their momma.

Being bathed in comfort and love had become foreign to me, the older I got. My nightly routine changed from fireflies in the field with momma to picking up numerous empty bottles of Jack Daniels cradled in her passed-out arms.

I swear momma loved that damn bottle of whiskey more than me. It made me mad. I often took those empty whiskey bottles and smashed them. One by one, they broke up against the side of our trailer, until the shards laid splayed out like a sea of shiny little diamonds.

But there was nothing shiny or beautiful about those shattered fragments of smelly glass. It always amazed me how, despite being destroyed, each individual piece of glass held onto the distinct putrid aroma of chaos and pain it caused. The unmistakable scent of whiskey. Almost as tightly as momma's stranglehold of memories she tried in vain to drink away but never could.

Momma never once noticed the piles of busted glass I had created. She never awoken from drunken slumbers while the bottles hit the side of the trailer. She just staggered over the shards as if they were a crystal carpet laid out especially for her. Momma staggered over everything in life, including me.

I often wondered about my daddy while I stared upwards at the darkened sky full of lit bums from the fireflies.

'Did my daddy leave momma and me because he wanted a boy instead of a girl? Did we ever pass each other by on the street? Did he like double-scooped mint chocolate chip ice cream, too? Did I have half-brothers or sisters? Did he ever think about me? Did he miss me?'

Questions about my daddy bounced daily inside my little wispy blonde-haired coated brain matter like a 1970's pinball machine. I always seemed to have an endless supply of metaphoric quarters to keep those thoughts banging and clanging for hours on end.

Ping-ting-bonk-zonk-thwapp!

At the end of the day, I tilted and drifted off to sleep until the next morning where more pinball quarters, more thoughts and endless wonders resumed.

I never knew anything about my daddy. The color of his eyes. The color of his hair. If he was tall? Short? Did he smell like an expensive cologne? Or reek of cheap whiskey and cigarettes like momma?

I never knew his last name. Momma refused to speak it. She made certain the hospital etched her family name, *Jackson*, on my birth certificate when I was born so I could never find him.

I thought, '*Was my daddy even the man you thought was my daddy, momma?*'

Before things got worse for me, whenever I saw fireflies twinkling, I embraced feelings of warmth and love from the glow of their projected light. I desperately craved for momma to love me. But she drifted further away, on purpose, the older I got. Fireflies had soon taken her place and became the closest I ever got to knowing that type of loving, motherly warmth.

I noticed when their lights vanished, horrible, empty feelings of abandonment immediately took root. My soul felt strangled by an old witch's withered, decrepit hand whose bones were brittle and yet, strong enough to inflict pain and drain the breath straight out of your body simultaneously.

I was so starved for love and affection. Unfortunately, I failed to understand back then the difference between right love and affection, and wrong love and affection. I was just a kid. How could I have known? Sadly, I would come to realize the difference.

I despised the loneliness. Momma knew my feelings but did not care or she would have changed. I would have taken priority in her life over her precious whiskey. But her precious Jack was the favored child. There was nothing I could do about it.

I often begged momma to stay with me in our rundown trailer and not leave me alone. *Nope.* Momma loved three things. Well, four. But the fourth one she dared not admit. Not even in a drunken whisper to God.

Momma loved: whiskey, the company of men, herself, and my daddy. She always acted as if she hated my daddy. But she never fooled me. I might have been young. I might have been naïve and a bit uneducated. But observations and common sense were my keen traits. I was convinced momma never got over my daddy who walked out on us when I was still in diapers.

My daddy's abrupt departure was the reason why she drank herself into a nightly stupor. It was the reason why she chose to run around with so many men. It was a deception to try and forget something that could not be forgotten.

Over time, I learned you cannot forget things embedded so deep inside the heart. It will forever remain until you acknowledge its existence.

Momma never could deal with anything. She held onto her heartache caused by my daddy until the day she kissed Jack goodbye with a hearty exhale of her alcohol-riddled breath.

Eventually, I got accustomed to momma disappearing for days at a time on drunken benders. I stopped begging her to stay. I knew sooner or later she would return with a new guy in tow. Some low life she picked up at a bar. Her flirting with so many men was how we kept bills paid and food on the table. Even *Jack's* rent in her liver was paid for.

During her drunken benders, I was left alone, locked inside a rented, roach-infested trailer with nothing but stale generic brand cereal, cold water, broken crayons, a stack of old newspapers to color on and a half-busted television to watch on days it decided to work.

Our fridge was always empty. Momma did not like to cook. We ordered a lot of pizzas. Two cans of expired sweet peas covered in dust sat in the cupboards since we had moved into the trailer two years ago. They had been abandoned by the previous tenant. I felt everything in common with those unwanted cans of peas.

My loneliness was palpable. I begged momma relentlessly to stay whenever she tried to leave without me. But my complaints and hot tears repeatedly fell upon deaf ears.

I despised loneliness. What I despised even more was the male company she chose to entertain at our trailer. To me, those men were bandits who stole momma's attention away from where it should have been.

I loathed the heavy drinking she shared with those men. The drugs, too. Our trailer filled with so much cigarette smoke; I felt like a ship lost in the fog, as I navigated my way from my bedroom across the hall to our one and only bathroom.

Before long, drunken yells between momma and whatever man she brought home started up. Next, a door slam, followed by loud grunting and mattress spring squeaking sounds from the back bedroom.

Soon after, the front door opened, then slammed shut.

I always whispered, *"Good riddance, creep!"* when the man of the night exited.

Another night of hell, over. I finally rested my head on my stained pillow and curled up with a teddy bear I had fashioned together with newspaper, then stuffed with more newspaper, and held together with various sized rubber bands. I drifted off to sleep, just as the cockroaches had awoken to try and pry those old cans of peas open.

I loathed momma for not wanting to spend time with me. I believed it stemmed from my daddy who had left us. I reminded her of him. I never knew the man, so why did I care so much, too? I still care.

I further resented how momma acted as if she gave two shits if I existed or not. She treated me like I was some burden thrust into her life on purpose. She was the one who thrusted with my daddy and nine months later birthed me.

I never asked to be born. Why was I blamed for something I had no control over? Momma should have controlled that wandering vagina of hers the night she met my daddy. That's what she should have done. Then, I never would have existed, and she and *Jack* could have ridden off into the whiskey sunset together. Mouth to bottle just as she always wanted it to be.

Momma made no secret in later years about how much she resented my existence. Especially the years I blossomed like a pure, white gardenia, while the drinking she had done, turned her into an old, ugly, weed.

I never resented my existence, despite the horrible way momma rejected me, until my seventh birthday.

From that day forward, I struggled to navigate through life.

My seventh birthday was a personal introduction into the world of dirty, nasty-minded men who were unwillingly and repeatedly thrusted into my mind, body, and soul… without my permission.

The same men momma entertained inside our trailer. The same men she used for money to pay our rent, cigarettes and her precious *Jack*. The same men who used her in return, only for their own specific needs.

The same legion of men who decided on my seventh birthday was my turn to reimburse their dues.

My self-hatred grew with each passing rotation of the sun, each inappropriate touch and each forced drag down the hallway to the back bedroom.

I tried to make sense of the new dark feelings which moved into my heart and evicted what small amount of light which had remained throughout momma's rejection and abuse. Dark feelings which festered from within until the third trimester when they were born on my seventh birthday.

Dark feelings that scratched and clawed up my insides something awful. Dark feelings that tore my soul apart piece by piece. Dark feelings that yearned to be unleashed with a retaliation cocooned within an unspeakable wrath.

I never allowed those feelings to escape. I fought to hold them inside. I feared what or who I would become should they have ever broken free.

Happy Hellish Birthday to Me!

Light.

Dark.

Light.

Dark.

Light.

Dark.

I sat in a three-legged dining room chair, captivated by the flickered glow of seven birthday candles momma had lit with her classic Bic lighter. The blue and white striped candles had been thoughtlessly jammed through the creamy chocolate frosting of the store-bought vanilla cake. Some candles leaned left. Some leaned right. Some had nearly fallen off with loose frosting still attached.

I watched as momma lit the candles in the kitchen and then carried the lopsided cake into the dining room.

I thought, 'S*he loves me and really wants me to have a Happy Birthday, after all.'*

The cake was the most beautiful cake my eyes had ever seen. It had big pink roses and green vines swirled all around it. The imperfect cake was still beautiful until momma dropped it hard onto the tabletop before me on purpose.

The organized roses slanted, same as the candles. I knew what the dropped cake meant. Momma was furious with me.

"Well go on. What the hell are you waiting for?" She bent forward and crudely hissed into my ear, *"Your daddy?"*

I said nothing. I feared an undeserved slap to the face. Great birthday, huh.

"Make a wish before you turn eight." She then kicked my three-legged chair hard enough I grabbed onto the edge of the table or risked falling.

I was dumbfounded as I watched momma empty the rest of *Jack* down her throat. I had not extended an invitation to Mr. Daniels nor momma's latest slimeball man, to my birthday party. I was upset and disappointed.

Momma met the burly biker at one of her regular watering holes. The mountain man looking dirtbag, smelled of an alcohol, motor oil and stale cigarette combo. He stayed in our trailer for the past week and leered at me every chance he had. Momma caught him staring at me a few times but said nothing. She did not want to spoil what she believed was 'a good thing'.

'Another drunken loser that smelled worse than the loser before him. Perfect.'

I knew his lustful looks tossed in my direction fueled momma's anger. But it was not my fault. I did nothing to entice him. If anything, she should have been angry at him, not me. I wanted him to leave after the first night. I begged her to make him go. But she would not kick him out. So now I paid the price for her poor choice. We had even fought about it the night before my birthday party while he was in the shower.

"Dammit, Tobi! I'm entitled to some happiness in my life! Just shut up and mind your business and leave him be. Ya hear?" She then grabbed my face hard with her right hand. I thought my chipmunked cheeks were going to explode from the pressure.

"You understand what I am telling you? Don't look at him. Don't prance your tiny ass around him with them little green terrycloth shorts of yours on neither. Ya hear me. You steer clear out of his sight."

"*Yes, momma,*" I whispered back. I felt defeated.

Since our discussion, I had done everything momma asked of me. I stayed out of his sight as best I could. I spent most of my time hidden away in my bedroom where I drew pictures on top of old newspapers. I even peed in an old whiskey jar to avoid running into him on my way to the bathroom.

'Piss on you, Jack. Take that!'

My attempts to avoid him were apparently not enough for momma. I landed in her crosshairs based on how she treated my cake. And me, with that hard, unprovoked kick to the chair.

I had been bored for days prior while locked away inside my bedroom alone. And yet, it was not enough. I had laid on my ancient, stained mattress momma and I had fetched from a dumpster and colored on top of things I had already colored. I had no mirror to talk back to myself for company. No dresser for my clothes to rearrange. No real toys. Nothing a girl my age should have. She always spent any money gained on booze, cigarettes., occasionally bills, pizza and men. Hardly anything on me.

One time when momma had left for days with another man she had met, I went down to the dumpster and found a pile of romance books near a trash bag riddled with flies. I snuck those raunchy books into my room. I tried to read the books, but I failed to understand most of the words. So, I made up stories as I turned the pages. When I grew bored of reading, I removed the covers and made a set of cardboard dolls to play with.

For the past three days I had done my best to avoid her biker dirtbag. But I noticed if I left my room, even for a glass of water, there he was. He would just stare at me like a starving snake to a cute bunny rabbit. I wished he had slithered out of our trailer for good before my birthday.

I longed to spend my seventh birthday with only momma. I missed the time we once spent together when I was younger. I had even dreamt of doing fun things mothers and daughters do. Shopping. Going to the zoo. Stuff I had seen on our half-working television and also from pictures in the magazines I had colored over. I would have especially loved to go in the field with the fireflies.

'To see the warm glow of the fireflies and feel the warmth of momma's desire to spend time with me…the perfect birthday. But it was not to be.'

I remained frozen in the three-legged chair with my ruined cake before me. I tried to conjure up a wish before blowing out the candles. I was deep in thought when I felt the hairs of the motorcycle dirtbag's brown beard brush up against my right cheek.

He whispered into my ear, *"You sure are pretty. Even prettier than your momma."* He then kissed my cheek. *"Don't tell her what I said. It's our special secret."* I shivered and hoped momma had not seen him close to me. If so, the blame would have landed square on my shoulders.

I closed my eyes and wished with all my might for the motorcycle dirtbag to have disappeared so I could spend my birthday with momma, only. My grape scented *Kool-Aid* breath blew forth and extinguished each of the seven candles. When I opened my eyes, much to my horror, momma was passed out face down on the table next to the chocolate ice cream box.

'Happy Hellish Birthday, Tobi!'

I will forever detest my seventh birthday. I will never forget one single detail about the very day I fell into a pit of darkness and despair. No hope in sight.

I recalled, *'To this day, I still see the bright yellow paper tablecloth covered with giant painted green, red, and blue balloons. My lopsided rose chocolate iced cake with the seven half-melted blue and white striped candles nestled on top. A container of chocolate ice cream melted over the sides of its cardboard container and headed towards momma's right arm. And three presents wrapped in paper towels sat in a chair, yet to be opened. I don't believe they ever were. Momma threw them away in a heated rage once she found out about the motorcycle dirtbag and me.'*

At seven years old, I became an internal prisoner trapped inside a jail constructed of pure pain, stuck in a repetitive, endless cycle of abuse propagated by momma's turnstile of degenerate boyfriends. Men who desired to assault me once momma was passed out drunk.

My seventh birthday was when the nightmare had begun. A nightmare I feared would never end. Sometimes I did not want it to end. Sometimes I felt like I deserved it. All of it. I now thought of myself as the very trash she had always said I was to the world. And maybe she had been right about me all along. Facts do not lie. Momma did not want me. My daddy did not want me. Both had thrown me away.

But the drunken men momma brought around. They yearned for me. Even if, they too, disposed of me like trash afterwards. Despite the revulsion of their touches, I experienced what it felt like to be wanted by someone. But I knew it was all wrong. I continually contradicted myself. When momma's men were done with me, I held myself tight, rocked back and forth and whispered, *'Why? Why? Why? Why did they want to hurt me? Why didn't momma stop them from hurting me? Why didn't momma take my side when I told her what they had done to me while she was passed out drunk?'*

The *'whys'* always hit my heart like sharp darts.

Bullseye.

Bullseye.

Bullseye.

And, yet never got answered.

Momma never spoke a word to me after the first *'incident'* with her dirtbag biker man happened. Not one word. Not one apology. She never offered a lame reason or pathetic excuse for his rotten behavior. She acted like it never took place until he was gone. Instead of comfort or protection from further harm, she instead glared at me and then coated her esophagus with as much whiskey as possible to swim in a sea of denial that her man wanted me more than he wanted her.

'Why?'

There were countless times I cupped my tiny hands tightly over my ears to silence out the sound of the screams which emanated from within me while momma's creepy men touched me. My inner cries were so loud, and yet, they went unheard, as much as my outer cries did.

I wanted momma to help me, but she never would. She heard only the soft croons of *Jack Daniels* as he tickled sweet words into her ears to continue drinking.

Sometimes I sang a song inside my head to drown out the sounds of my inner screams. One of my favorites was a song I heard from one of momma's records:

California Dreamin'
by the Mamas & the Papas

All the leaves are brown (all the leaves are brown)
And the sky is gray (and the sky is gray)
I've been for a walk (I've been for a walk)
On a winter's day (on a winter's day)
I'd be safe and warm (I'd be safe and warm)
If I was in L.A. (if I was in L.A.)
California dreamin' (California dreamin')
On such a winter's day

One day, after another of her men had done me over, I worked up the nerve and asked her, "Why do you let your men do those things to me?"

Momma stared at me, then said, "Ya must have asked for it," before she poured herself another drink, with a shot of added look of disgust aimed in my direction.

"Quit your cryin' and blubberin' and go get cleaned up. He didin't mean nothin' by it. And even if he did, that's just what men do. Get used to it."

"Get used to it?" I would whisper under my breath while I washed their unwanted touches off using stolen gas station soap. '*Never!*'

Regardless of how I felt, I always did as momma asked. But I struggled with the *why* of it all. Mothers protected their children from hungry wolves. They did not chuck them straight into their snarled jaws like raw meat.

I often pondered, *'What had I done to make momma willingly hand me over to those ravenous wolves without care? What happened to the days when we used to lie in the field together looking at fireflies? Maybe momma allowed her men to do what they did to me because my loud cries helped drown out her own silent ones.'*

I also thought, *'Maybe momma missed my daddy. Maybe she still loved him and because of that, would change her mind and not want those men messing with her more than they already had done. So, she let them mess with me instead so that way she could still get their money to pay bills and buy booze, pizza and cigarettes. You know, the things which mattered most to her. Or maybe she was flat jealous because those men used her to get to me. To them she was the trash. I was the treasure they hunted for. I never felt like a real gold treasure. More like fools' gold. A fool for putting up with it.'*

I often prayed my daddy would return home where he belonged. I did not really know how to pray, so maybe that is why it never came true. I tried to mimic what I had heard the television preachers speak about on our half-working television and made the rest up as the wheels inside my head sputtered, backfired, and turned.

I prayed my daddy would burst through the front door and rescue me each time I was dragged to the master bedroom. While I kicked and screamed at the top of my lungs, my eyes always locked hard on momma. Messy haired. Her arms clutched around an empty whiskey bottle. The one and only thing she loved most in the world. Besides my daddy.

She would occasionally yell out in a drunken slur, "*Worf-less pisssss of shit. Go on then. Leave. We don' need you. We don' want you. Jussssss go!*"

My tiny fingers grabbed in vain at pieces of old, faded wallpaper already peeled from the wall of our dilapidated trailer. The paper was too weak to stop me from being dragged to the back bedroom by those men. But I tried my best to stop them anyway I could think of.

Meanwhile, as my horror began, there was momma, passed out drunk. Her limp body sprawled about on our floral, liquid-stained second-hand couch. Both legs gapped wide apart. Soiled, urine-stained panties wrapped loosely 'round her boney ankles. Open for business. Yet, no customers were interested in entering through her crusty, unkempt door.

I would yell at the top of my lungs, "Momma! Help! Please! Make him let me go!" Only to be met with, "*Shuuuuu up you little brat! Stop your whining! I'm tryinnnn' to sleep!*"

Soon, a loud slam of the bedroom door sounded off, "BAM!"

My eyes remained fixated on the doorknob. "*Please turn. Please. Please,*" I routinely begged in a faint whisper. But the knob only turned when the assault was over. Never before.

Afterwards, I staggered back down the hallway and into my bedroom where I tried to pretend nothing happened. I vomited sometimes in the corner of my room before I then crawled into my own bed, sore and broken.

Meanwhile, momma remained passed out on the couch with a man who had just violated her daughter sleeping like a demented version of *Goldilocks* in her bed in the back bedroom. A smile of satisfaction smeared across his face.

I dreamt about my daddy. I imagined he kicked down the bedroom door, pulled that rotten man off me and beat him into a pile of nothing but bones and bloody guts. I gleefully jumped up and down on his busted-up bones and screamed, "I hate you! I hate you! I hate you!". But it never happened. My daddy never rescued me, except in my dreams. And momma never stopped them. Always in reality.

I was trapped inside a bad dream only hell was constructed of. I was alone. I was scared. I was confused. And I lacked a map of hope to escape from the burning flames which sizzled and cracked and hissed right beneath my feet. I soon realized no one was going to rescue me from this horrendous life. No one.

I was trapped inside a jar like a captured firefly who longed to be free to fly again. Only its captor was so entranced by their own desires the flickering insect offered, they selfishly tossed aside the insect's needs, where the insect eventually quit blinking. It's light extinguished forever.

The older I got the more men wanted to make the letter J for me instead of with momma. I never wanted their disgusting J's. But what I wanted mattered not to anyone. I despised the letter J. I refused to pronounce it in school when we had to recite our ABC's. I would cough or burp if I had to. Anything to avoid speaking it.

As I lay on my back in a darkened field covered in fireflies and attempted to recapture childhood solace, I shouted out the alphabet, letter by letter. "ABCDEFGHI…" When it came to the letter J, I stuck my middle finger up towards the sky instead. *"Screw you letter J. I hate you!"*

I continued to blossom into a teenager. By then, I accepted my daddy would never return to save me. I accepted momma was a drunken whore whose men would never leave me be. All I wanted to do was finish school, leave momma and her nasty men, and never look back. But things do not always work out the way we planned.

The warmth and comfort I once sought in the firefly's soft glow had all but disappeared. They no longer provided me with comfort or safety. I had grown cold. Hard-hearted. Hateful. Withdrawn. Empty. I felt absolutely nothing …until the day I fell into the *dirt*.

Blue-collared Times

Nothing felt freer than a ride in a pickup truck with the windows down. My shag-cut, dirty blonde hair whipping wildly about in the wind. My puffy cheeks, rosy with color. The taste of the cool breeze as it playfully danced across my protruding pink tongue. *"Hmmm…sweet."* I loved to open my mouth wide and shout, *"Woohoo!"* at the top of my lungs.

On a crisp early morning, I enjoyed that simple pleasure from the past. All thanks to a blue-collared John I tricked before his shift at the local garage started. He was a regular and a mechanic, but never great with his hands. After our business transaction was completed, I had asked to hitch a ride to North Nebraska Avenue.

North Nebraska Avenue was a cesspool back when I was a child of the streets. The road was peppered with car washes, strip joints, auto-repair stores, used appliance stores, a greasy-spoon diner, and several second-hand furniture stores. It was also a street where the occasional meat pole surprise was discovered hidden underneath certain ladies' skirts by the untrained eye of amorous tourists. North Nebraska Avenue was a well-known area where twenty dollars got any filthy desires fulfilled.

Once the mechanic's truck engine turned over, my ears tuned into the sound of a familiar song which played in static waves from a set of old speakers nestled behind the front bench seat. The Outlaws. I only knew it because momma used to play their records.

Green Grass and High Tides
By the Outlaws

In a place you only dream of
Where your soul is always free
Silver stages, golden curtains
Filled my head, plain as can be
As a rainbow grew around the sun
All my stars of love who died
Came from somewhere beyond the scene you see
These lovely people played just for me

I mumbled to myself, *"Momma and good old Jack Daniels were outlaws same as Bonnie and Clyde. Inseparable and insufferable."*

"You say something, sweetheart?" the blue-collared John asked.

I pointed forward with my right index finger. "Nope. Let's go."

That raise of my right arm immediately told me I needed a shower. I realized I had worn the same white crop top, cut-off jean shorts and busted down flipflops for two days in a row.

My hair was greasy.

My make-up smeared.

My skin felt grungy.

I basically stunk.

Deodorant was a long-forgotten luxury since those nice church ladies handed out bags of personal hygiene items to the working girls on North Nebraska Avenue over two weeks ago. Most times money earned went towards drugs and food. Deodorant and soap rarely made the list because, *dirt* always came first.

I truly cared less how I looked or smelled. I struggled to manage with good personal hygiene since childhood. I remained nasty back then on purpose to deter momma's boyfriends so they would leave me be. It never worked. They never seemed to mind. But I continued to do it regardless.

If I could not afford a motel room or find a John willing to let me use their shower, I got creative. I used gas station sinks and cold watered garden hoses I found in yards. I despised the cold water, but it got the job done so I was presentable enough to work for the sole purpose to score *dirt*. My only true objective.

I hung my head out the window and yelled, *"Woohoo!"* as the truck zoomed down the road towards North Nebraska Avenue.

I rustled my hair with my right hand before I pulled myself back inside the truck's cab.

The morning sun comforted my soul as I watched it glisten off the blonde hairs of my right arm, which I had rested on the door frame. I closed my eyes and enjoyed the sensation of the wind as it playfully rushed between my fingers.

My mind wandered.

I had dreamt of being a nurse. When I was a kid, I would cover my newspaper teddy bear in bandages made from perfume sample cards I found in magazines folks in our trailer park threw out. I made them stick with gum I stole from the gas station. Sometimes I made arm or leg splints from cut up cereal boxes. I used whatever I could find.

Unfortunately, my dreams were put on hold and then for a while, forgotten altogether. I had to quit school during my sophomore year to take care of momma. Her true love, *Mr. Daniels*, had beaten her liver something awful. She got sick. In the blink of a firefly's glow, overnight, momma had become the child. I, the parent.

Momna now wetted the bed. Vomited on herself. But not because she had been sexually assaulted like me. It was because of cirrhosis. Despite all I sacrificed, she remained the same evil, cruel witch who never apologized for what her disgusting men had done to me.

I used to think, '*Life's cruel to some more than others, I suppose. But life also evens the score, I suppose sometimes, too.*'

"Checkmate, huh, momma," I spitefully hissed into her ear, when I yanked Jack from her grasp.

I controlled when she and *Jack* spent time with one another. She had become too weak to hold on to *Jack* like in the past. But there were times, even as the disease took a stronger hold, momma managed enough strength to land slaps across my face.

She would shout, "Whore! You made those men want you more than they ever wanted me."

I never dared utter a response. I allowed her to hit, spit, yell, curse at me. I granted permission for her to treat me like the shit she always believed I was. She was often in and out of delusions. It was pointless to fight back with words or hands. She was never going to be sorry. I had to accept it. So, I took her abuse, not just with a grain of salt, but the whole damn block.

I resented giving up my dream and sacrificing more of my life for her. She never wanted me. Maybe my life and her love for me would have differed had my daddy stuck around. But I would never know. It was pointless to wonder further, so I stopped and accepted my fate. And hers, too.

Sometimes I secretly enjoyed those contentious moments between momma and me. I loved to piss her off on purpose. The same way she loved to hurt me from past to present for no reason.

I relished watching those flames of hatred erupt and flicker inside her blue pupils like a forest fire out of control. Those hearty slaps she landed across my cheeks, despite being feeble.

Things always came to a head when I denied her the opportunity to wrap her lips around *Mr. Daniels* and drink him down.

"I should do it you know. Let you and *Jack* be together around the clock. The sooner you're both gone from my life, the better."

"You bitch! Give him to me!" She would then lunge for the bottle, which I always yanked just out of her reach in time.

I watched her struggle to grab the bottle as a form of payback for each man she had allowed to touch me. I knew it was wrong, but the anger I carried inside somehow made it alright. No guilt.

Momma was dying. She became even more delusional as time marched on. Her liver was shutting down. Inside her mind, *Jack Daniels* was all she had left in the world. The only one who understood her. The only one who loved her. The only one who never left her. Yet, she failed to realize that in the end he was the one who killed her.

I never counted. Nor did my efforts to do right by her, either. I hoped we would heal from those old, festered wounds before she passed on. The closer she got to death, the more I wanted to savor every moment with momma I had left. Sounds odd, I know. I failed to understand it all myself. She never protected me, showed no love or compassion, treated me like a burden and never wanted me. I hated her for everything, but I loved her, too. It was unavoidable. She was my mother.

The endless arguments that took place inside my head.

'Man! Fuck her!'

'No! Do right by her even though she did wrong by you.'

Back and forth.

Back and forth.

Over and again ad nauseum.

There were no more men since momma had become bedridden. Only *Mr. Daniels*, the apple of her eye. And I, the worm.

I thought, *'Shame she was not a fan of Tequila. Maybe then I would have had a shot at being in her good graces.'*

Because the men had stopped, so, too, had the money. It was not long before I was the one forced to hit the streets and seduce men for their money just like momma had done. I had no choice. Momma's medical bills had to be paid. I was not old enough to get a normal paying job. Welfare never paid enough to keep a roof over our heads and food in the fridge. I resented momma even more for I had evolved into a carbon copy of her. I never wanted that for my life. Ever!

In her final months on earth, I took what abuse I could from momma; verbally, emotionally, and even physically. I took both the bitter and the sweet. The sweet being the one and only time she said the word *"please"* when she asked for *Jack's* company while watching a game show on our half-working television set.

"Screw you, Jack!" I mumbled.

"What was that you said, sweetheart?" the mechanic asked.

I immediately snapped out of my past at the sound of his voice.

"Nothing. Keep driving."

The mechanic reached over and casually placed his right hand on top of my left knee. I cringed and shot him a look that implied, *Take your damn hand off my thigh or I swear you aren't getting it back!*

He ignored my look and kept his hand rested firmly on my knee, as if it were a stick shift. I turned my gaze away from his lustful stare and looked out the window.

I fought the urge to punch him in the face. Honest I did. I wanted to punch him so hard his head broke the glass on his side of the window from the velocity and power of my fist. It was an automatic reflex from what I had gone through growing-up. I felt helpless for so long, but not anymore. I now felt powerful in my own twisted imagination.

So strange how I felt violated by the touch of his hand on my knee, especially after the naughty things we did fifteen minutes prior. But the ride he had offered me to North Nebraska Avenue was not included as part of our business. That was over. Services rendered. I allowed his hand to stay put only because I really needed the ride. Otherwise, I would have bent his fingers backward until he pulled the truck over and let me out.

I compartmentalized events that took place in my life. Work. Getting high. Being alone. It became my knack from childhood experience. I learned to develop different coping mechanisms for each situation.

The life I lived on North Nebraska Avenue to support my habit of *dirt* and my failed attempts at erasing my past literally caused me to vomit. I had to do what I loathed doing since I turned seven years old. But there was no other way I could endure the streets or life in general without doing it. So, I did what I had to do to survive.

Business was business.

Nothing personal about it.

I got paid.

They got service.

I literally checked out during a job.

I knelt for Johns.

I laid down for Johns.

I got down on all fours for Johns.

I did a lot of odd and repulsive things for Johns.

The men had their fun.

I shivered the entire time.

I forever fought the urge to barf during it.

Release would finally happen.

They'd get dressed.

Sometimes I earned extra cash.

So long asshole!

Next.

After enough dates, enough money, quitting time.

Off to meet my dealer.

Score some *dirt*.

Next stop?

Somewhere secluded to bang the newly purchased *dirt* into my body and forget all of it.

My torments erased until my next needed fix.

Lather.

Rinse.

Repeat.

Day after day.

I had it all under control.

Or so I thought.

But who was I kidding?

Only me – that's who.

The blue-collared John mistakenly thought I owed him free touches for the ride. I strongly disagreed, but kept my mouth shut. It was very important I reached North Nebraska. I fought the urge to punch the side of his semi-gray, whiskery face and instead, wished for a steady stream of green lights for the remainder of the ride.

'Dammit!'

Red light.

I shook my head side to side. I was disappointed.

'Why does the universe hate me so much?'

His greasy, lecherous hand crept up my bare leg like a drunken beach crab. I shuddered, but dared not look down. My eyes bore a hole through that retched red light. I was pissed. Nothing in life was free. Everything came with a price. A lesson momma and *Mr. Daniels* taught me all too well. How in the hell could I forget?

Now that I was older, I mistakenly believed the tables had mystically turned in my favor. I had the power. I continued to loath men. They still longed to make the letter 'J' with me. Nevertheless, I took their money after they got what they wanted just to stay buried in *dirt*.

The truth?

The only difference between the men in the past versus current was where the money got spent. In the past I needed money for momma's care and bills. I needed it now for my drug habit. I was in the same spot. Nothing changed. I just fooled myself into believing otherwise. But when I was a child, the exchange between us was different.

I thought to myself, *'You wanted to make the letter 'J' with me? Well, it now came at a hefty price. No more freebies in the back bedroom like in the past.'*

"Finally," I blurted out, as the light turned green, and the classic truck lurched forward.

"Sorry, darlin'. Need to have a mechanic look at this old gal's clutch. She sticks sometimes." He then winked. I suppose he thought his lame joke *(because he was a mechanic)* would win him a bonus.

"Whatever," was all I replied.

I did what I had to do to survive on the streets and support my drug habit. Still, it never made what Johns' did to me in cars, alleyways, and motels seem right.

Sometimes I thought about their women during our encounters. At home. Clueless. I thought about how they would feel if they found out how nasty their men truly were both the dark and the light. I never should have wondered or cared. Somewhere in the back of my mind, it always gnawed at my conscience for unknown reasons.

Maybe because of my daddy. How momma's broken heart over him leaving caused her to drink herself to death and go through men like toilet paper. I often wondered if my daddy was a John to a girl like me. If that was the reason momma forbade his name to be spoken while breath remained in her body. She never told me anything about him. To this day, I still do not know his name or if I have his nose or ears.

I glanced at the blue-collared John. He returned my glance with a coy grin. His fingers had begun to trace tiny circles, round and around on my inner left thigh. I looked away. Repulsed.

Funny thing. In that very moment it dawned on me the word 'John' started with the letter 'J'.

I shook my head and whispered, *"Well, shit Bug. How come you never connected the dots on that one before? Idiot!"*

Countless horrible things happened to me before momma died. And even worse afterwards. I gave up my dream of going back to school to get my GED so I could then go to college and become a nurse.

Dirt had me firm within its filthy clutches. And I had *dirt* firm within my grimy soul. The same as momma and *Jack Daniels*. Perhaps the rotten apple had not fallen so far from the polluted tree after all.

By my late teens, I was buried deep in the *dirt*. A bonafide junky and whore who relied on men to take care of her, but only if she 'took care of them' first. I had, without question, nor reservation or even hesitation, become my momma.

'Holy Hell!'

The only difference between momma and me though, I preferred the sweet kiss of heroin over whiskey.

During times when I raged with anger over momma's love for booze over me, I stole mini bottles of *Jack Daniels* from a low-rent liquor store and threw them hard against an abandoned building.

"Fuck you, *Jack*! I hope the two of you are happy partying the night away with Satan! She's all yours! Always was! Always will be!"

As the ground got drunk from the countless shattered whiskey bottles, I banged *dirt* into my arm. I had to numb up the repetitive cycle of childhood heartache. The past voices. The smells. The sounds. My cries for help when no one listened. All of it.

There were others like me on the streets. We were a dime a dozen. Ones who had been abused and even worse. Then there were those who somehow escaped the abuse, the drugs, the alcoholism before it consumed them. They were sober, healed and free.

Why couldn't that be me, too?

I already knew the answer before the question was even asked.

Because you're weak.

I found it easier to get wasted and avoid the torment, than to fight back. I was never told I had strength by anyone in my life. Therefore, I believed myself to be weak as a result. Too weak to abandon whatever horrific life I was born into. Too weak to walk away from poor life choices. Too weak period.

The thing about being a junky, I never felt responsible for most of the crappy stuff I did to myself or to others. It was much easier to point the finger of blame outward than inward.

I knew I was not strong. Momma made sure to shower me with continual, venomous affirmations about being weak and pathetic. "You were so weak while inside me, you couldn't even muster the guts to give me the morning sickness."

Most women appreciated an easy pregnancy without puking. But not momma. She resented me for not making her sick.

'What?'

I missed her presence in my life sometimes. But only sometimes. Odd right? To miss the one who was supposed to love and take care of you. But instead, turned into the one who abused you. The one who allowed others to abuse you, too.

How was it even possible to miss things about her? To care? To cry over her not being around anymore? But I did. I hated it when my heart got sentimental for her.

You want to know something? It had been a long time since I saw a firefly. And if I were honest, for the first time in my life I did not give one flying shit about it.

'Screw the light!'

Two Droplets Meet

To survive life on the streets you either kept to yourself or joined a *family*. A group of folks from different walks of life who looked out for one another. They were the ones who got treated like lepers by society and loved ones. A street family that was comprised of people who either chose the wrong road or were forced to live it due to unforeseen circumstances.

I did not have a street family for a long time. My real family, momma, had died in my eyes long before she took her last breath. The only other blood relative was my daddy. But I did not know his name and therefore had no idea where to find him. For all I knew, he was dead, too.

'Where are you at daddy? I wish I could find you.'

In the beginning, I kept to myself. I trusted no one. Other whores. Johns. Scraggly alley cats. Scurrying cockroaches. No one. The only exception, my dealer, Tiny. And only because he provided an escape from my excruciating mental and emotional pain. I never feared buying bad *dirt* from Tiny. If I did, the worst that would have happened was death. Pain exterminated. Effective immediately.

'Who would care if I died anyways? No one.'

I felt so laid back about death, practically welcomed it, until an unexpected encounter with a wannabe flowerchild named Chloe happened.

'That damn hippie!'

My mind, my heart, everything changed the moment I looked into those brown doe-shaped eyes of hers. I saw trust for the first time. I saw something I desired my whole life. A sister. Family. I was home.

The rain poured down from the skies, something fierce the day we met. I thought, *'God, you sure are doing your darndest to wash away all the filth polluting Nebraska Avenue, huh?'*

It was crowded underneath the small bridge sandwiched between East Hollywood Street and Grant Avenue, where eleven of us had gathered for shelter during the unexpected thunderous storm.

The air beneath the bridge was stagnant and hung heavy with various scents of *dirt*, crack, marijuana, cigarettes, and methamphetamine. The combined smoke from them all danced about in the atmosphere like a cryptic fog. Other aromas dodged their way between the smoke. Alcohol. Urine. Feces. Dried vomit on clothing. Bad breath. And loads of rancid body odor.

We were crammed together like an expired swollen tin can of sardines about to erupt at any moment. United momentarily for shelter from the rain and varied fixes for our private individual pain.

I could hardly breathe underneath the bridge without an achieved contact high from the haze generated by the heavy drug use by everyone.

I heard the whooshing sound of tires as cars passed by up above. To me, each car was a potential John and a lost chance to earn dough for *dirt*.

It was pointless to pout over opportunities lost. I accepted the clouds were going to piddle down rain until they decided to quit. Based on the booming thunder, it was going to be a while.

'Just make the best of it, Bug,' I whispered underneath my breath.

I positioned myself close to the edge of the concrete floor. I was nearly shoulder to shoulder with the steady stream of wetness that cascaded over the side of the bridge. Even though I periodically got battered by dirty street water, it beat sitting shoulder to shoulder with the other strung-out, foul-smelling sardines.

All I could think was *'Man, some of ya'll need to get out in the rain and clean up. You stink.'* But who was I to judge. I stank, too.

Endless droplets of water splashed hard to the ground and then sprayed onto my face like gentle kisses from up above. My mind trailed off.

I tried to convince myself in a moment of weakness that God cared about me, and I was being baptized. All of my sins forgiven. Despite never having caused most of them. But I quickly shook my head side to side and muttered, *"If He cared, He never would have let those men…Ah, forget it."*

The smell under the bridge soon became too much. I prepared some *dirt* and then searched for a good vein. Due to frequent usage, a good vein was hard to find.

I normally refrained usage around others. If I were caught holding, people would beg, bargain, or if desperate enough, try and kill me for my stash. The dependence on the drug normally determined the outcome.

I was in pain; mentally, physically, and emotionally. The usual. I was also bored. Plus, the trapped stench underneath the bridge was not doing my stomach or nostrils any favors, either. I needed to check out for a while. I chose to take the risk and soon thereafter, a hit of *dirt.*

The needle penetrated a vein between my ring and pinky finger. The dirt descended into my heart, mind, and soul. Within seconds any bad vibes churning around inside my body were silenced. I whispered, *"Finally."*

I laid down on my back, turned my head to the right and watched mud slide down the hillside before it spilled into the Hillsborough River below.

I thought about those individual raindrops. How they dropped from a cloud in the sky like tiny paratroopers, ready to work together with their squad once watery boots hit the ground. Upon touchdown, they temporarily joined together and pulled mud into the river where they were forever separated due to the river's rough current. Never reunited again. Only a carved path of destruction; uprooted plants, bits of trash and pebbles left scattered behind marked their once existence. Mission accomplished.

I thought how much the water droplets mirrored my life. Then I thought, *'Man. I'm so high…I feel low. What the hell did Tiny sell me?'*

My deep thoughts were unexpectedly interrupted when a fifteen-year-old girl tripped over my scabbed-up legs. I reached out my hand outward and grabbed her left hand before she joined the paratrooper droplets in the river.

"Whoa! You, okay?" I asked.

The tipsy girl regained her balance and replied, "Thanks for the save. I'm Chloe." She continued to hold onto my hand and stared into my soulless eyes.

I noticed two things about Chloe straight away. A tattoo of a peace sign on her middle finger. I thought, *'Ironic, predictable and lame'.* A clear attempt to piss off her parents.

I also noticed both of her rail-thin arms were peppered with track marks. The sound of her twenty-plus, silver bangled bracelets on her left arm jingled like wind chimes when she finally released my hand.

"Bug," I casually replied, then lit a cigarette.

Chloe pointed at an area of empty graffitied concrete next to me. "Cool?"

I nodded.

From that day forward, Chloe and I were inseparable. Two paratrooper droplets, dropped onto the planet from different clouds, now merged underneath a smelly bridge during a storm. Only our mission was a path paved with a revolving door of justified self-destruction. Our meeting was a long-lost family reunion.

Chloe

Chloe was a skinny, peace-loving, hippy. She wore her straight mousey brown hair long and parted down the middle with five scattered medium-sized braids. A threaded hairband decorated with feathers dropped by wild blue jays, crows, and trinkets *(mostly pop tops linked with string)* hugged her head like a crown.

"So many feathers," she said and shook her head side to side. "Now I can fly high, Bug! Just like that song we heard outside the strip club the other night." She then spun in circles with her arms outstretched.

"What song are you talking about?"

"Fly robin fly! Up! Up! To the Ssssssky!"

"You remember that song? Seriously?"

"It's a great song."

"You're high. Come sit down, Chloe before you crash to the ground like a plane that's run out of gas," I said.

She stuck her bottom lip out and pouted. "I don't care what you say, Bug. I'm a robin! I can't sit. I must fly!" She resumed making circles.

Chloe and I took the day off from hustling to spend it at the park. I needed a break. Between the two of us, we earned enough money to score dirt for the next twenty-four hours.

We purposefully chose a small park where people rarely visited. No risk of hassles from Johns, cops, or families. The grass felt soft and serene underneath my feet, like an avocado-colored shag rug. I always wondered what shag carpet felt like after watching game shows on our half-working television set when I was a kid. The grass in the park was the closest I would ever come to knowing the answer.

The sun shone brightly, but with a gentle warmth, instead of its usual harsh heat. For once it was nice not to feel like an overcooked egg in a frying pan.

I playfully wiggled my toes in the grass. It felt amazing to be off my feet. Hell, even my knees. Even if only for one day. I could just be and enjoy those little things most take for granted. Simple, long forgotten things.

Chloe's repetitive spins started to make me ill.

"Hey, robin. You do realize you're only flying high thanks to the shit I scored from Tiny, right. It's not the feathers stuck on your bird-brained head or the song, either."

"I can be a robin if I want to, Bug. I can be anything I want to be. You're not my mom. You're not even my pimp. You can't tell me what to do." She spun around again out of pure spite.

"Whatever. But if you keep spinning like that, you're going to puke," I snapped back.

Chloe grinned and fell to the ground in a fit of dizziness wrapped in a blanket of laughter. "Doesn't matter what bird the feathers come from, Bug. Don't you get it?"

"Get what?" I was simultaneously intrigued and puzzled.

Chloe rolled onto her stomach, "Feathers are always able to fly."

"Not if they're not attached to, oh, I don't know, say a bird." I then tilted my head to the side and added a smirk.

Chloe shook her head side to side. "Not true." She sat up.

"Is that so? Then how is it possible, huh?"

"The wind, silly, Bug." Chloe reached over and rustled my hair.

I hated to be touched. Chloe knew it, too. But in that moment, I did not know if it was because of the softness of the grass beneath my feet. The comforting warmth of the sun which was like a mother's hug I had ached for my whole life. Or Tiny's grade a *dirt* which coursed through my veins. I welcomed Chloe's playful affection.

"Where do you come up with this 'feather's always fly crap', Chloe? I mean, I get the whole wind cradling a light feather and carrying it for a while before it falls back to the ground. But not heavy wings or tail feathers. Impossible without strong winds."

Chloe became flustered by my inability to unravel her twisted theory. In an exasperated tone, she semi-shouted, "Ugh! Bug!"

"Ugh, what, Chloe?"

She crawled over and got so close to my face; our noses made contact. "Doesn't matter what type of feather it is, Bug. They come from birds. Birds are free. Like you. Like me." She then screamed out at the top of her longs, "WE ARE FREE!"

"Free?" I took a drag off a cigarette I had lit, then exhaled. I was skeptical over her nonsense.

"Like feathers, we are free and will always fly. Whether we're attached to a bird or not."

I snickered. "I ain't for free. Sorry girl. And I'm too big for a bird to carry me, so…"

"Emu."

"Emu? Emu what?"

"An emu bird could carry you." She smiled as if she had been crowned the winner of a fight.

I reached my right hand outward and gently pushed Chloe on her face. She fell backwards like a bowling pin and remained flat on her back. She then reached over and placed her hand on my stomach. "I'm talking about your spirit, Bug."

I sarcastically nodded my head. "Okay. So now you're saying my spirit is like a feather, too? Got it." I wanted to shut her up. Less talking, more enjoying my high in silence.

"That's right!" Chloe clutched her own stomach tightly. "Feathers are like our spirits, Bug. Always free to fly wherever they want. Never being weighed down. You're got it, Bug! You've got it!"

I thought, *'Chloe's so naïve. I did not know whether to feel pity or anger towards her ignorance.'*

Truth was, Chloe and I were weighed down: oppression, depression, sexual assaults, molestation, battery, abandonment, starvation, addiction. The list was endless. So many boulders had been piled upon our 'free-flying feathered spirits' we may as well have resided in Bedrock, A.D. next to the *Rubbles* and the *Flintstones.*

'Note to self; find out what this shit was Tiny sold me and never give it to Chole again.'

"I think we need to get you something to eat, Chole."

Chloe jumped up and straddled over top of me and shook her feathered coated, semi-braided hair all over my face in a teasing manner. "Be free, Bug! Be free!"

"Get off me! That shit tickles hippy nutjob. You better not bust the cherry off my cigarette." She rolled off of me and laughed. I placed my cigarette between my teeth and attempted to recompose myself. I stood up. She did, too.

I noticed Chloe continuously dressed in two ways; a very tight T shirt with bell bottom jeans or a sundress with either vanilla-colored Go-Go boots or a pair of 1970's red Dr. Scholl's clogs she found at a Salvation Army store. How those clogs remained in better condition than my 2008 flipflops was a mystery Chloe and I debated countless times.

A warped Led Zeppelin IV cassette tape repeatedly played on a Walkman some trick gave to Chloe as payment for services rendered. She always had the *Walkman* turned on, the headphones slung around her neck.

I was pissed when I discovered she got played by a cheap John. We argued about it.

"Geez, Chloe! You're so clueless. It drives me insane sometimes. That jerk trick totally screwed you and then screwed you over. Don't you get it?" I pointed at the retro hunk of junk which blasted forth sound from the warped tape.

Chloe scoffed and turned up the volume. "I don't care what you say or think about my *Walkman*, Bug. *La, la, la, la!* One day, you'll see, Bug. I am going to go to California with flowers in my hair. Just like the song says."

I nearly choked on my cigarette, bewildered by her response to having been taken advantage of by someone. "You wear feathers in your hair birdbrain, not flowers."

With both hands placed firmly on her bony hips, Chloe glared at me with a look of loathing. "Flowers? Feathers? What's the difference? I'M. STILL. GOING."

"How? You can't even catch a ride for more than two blocks without getting carsick. California is like three thousand miles away."

"I'll take a bus."

"A bus?" I sarcastically pondered. "Right, because riding in a bus won't make you carsick, too."

She grew flustered. "Maybe I'll ride in a train or fly in a plane or ride a horse or a unicorn or a…" she trailed off. "Or maybe I'll just open up my arms and fly myself to California, like a bird."

Chloe dropped to the ground and pulled me down with her in the process. We both landed flat on our backs in the grass. It reminded me of those days when I used to lay out in the fields with momma watching the fireflies.

Chloe had closed her eyes and begun to sing the song, *Going to California* loudly and deliberately out of tune to irritate me in that sisterly way.

Before long, we acted like farm hogs, snorting with laughter and rolling around on our backs on the soft grass. We were tainted head to toe in the beautiful blissful trance *dirt* afforded us to feel. We equally shrieked out our own version of the song, *"with feathers in her hair…La, la, la, la! Not flowers!"*

Chloe believed in reincarnation. I never did. I was convinced once you died you turned to worm food. She also believed there was good in everyone. I disagreed there, too.

'Can you blame me after what I had been through since I was seven years old?'

Chloe thought she had currently been born in the wrong era. I never bought into Chloe's kooky reincarnation idea. I secretly feared coming back as a dung beetle.

'Just my luck to live, yet another life of shoveling shit up a treacherous hill. No thanks!'

Hell was where I belonged and what I deserved. No time jump adventures for me. I already knew my life was destined to be one of endless twists, turns and inappropriate touches.

Every day brought with it a new place or time era Chloe yammered on about with her reincarnation theory. I never knew what period to expect. But I did expect a headache by the end of each story.

"I think. No wait. I know I was once a pretty songbird in a past life," Chloe said in a melancholy tone.

"A songbird."

"Yeah, like a parrot. Maybe I was a parrot on a pirate's shoulder. *Arrrrrrrgh!*" She bobbed her head up and down in self-agreement. "Cool, right?"

I dismissed her notion with a nonchalant wave of my hand. "Impossible."

"Why impossible, Bug?" she replied, confused.

I snickered, "Because you can't carry a tune to save your ass. No way you could ever be a songbird of any kind. Besides, parrots are not songbirds."

"Yes, they are. I heard one whistling to the radio in a pet store once."

"Is that so?" I said with doubt and unbelief in my voice.

Chloe remained silent. I panicked because I had forgotten how sensitive she could be.

'Oh shit! Way to go, Bug.'

Instead of tears, much to my relief, Chloe released a snort-fueled laugh. "*Squawk!* Chloe wants some *dirt*. *Squawk!*"

"Well, Bug isn't holding anymore." I got up in her face and shouted back, "*Squawk!*"

Chloe pouted.

I planted a kiss on her dirty hippy-decorated forehead. I then reached into my shorts pocket and retrieved a smushed package of crackers from the Beans & Jellies Café.

"How about some stale, mashed-up crackers, instead?"

She responded with a quizzical look.

"Parrots like crackers. Right?" I taunted, waving a cracker back and forth in her face. "Chloe wants a cracker. You know she does."

Chloe opened her mouth wide like a baby bird. We both laughed as I tossed pieces of cracker at her mouth.

"*Squawk!* Bug missed. Try again! *Squawk!*"

The following week, Chloe imagined she was a red poppy flower in the fields of Afghanistan in another life. The flower in this kooky scenario was her – *of course*. I resisted the urge to roll my eyes while she spoke of being a poppy flower.

Chloe was harvested, made into *dirt*, and then smuggled into the United States to bring peace to someone who was in a lot of pain.

"You are so stupid high right now, Chloe."

"It's true, Bug. It's true. I swear it." She made the letter 'X' across her heart. "I swear. I was once a poppy flower."

"You were never a poppy flower, Chloe. What you are right now is stupid high."

Chloe looked at me peculiarly, then busted out laughing. "I am, aren't I?"

"Come on. Let's go get some real food to eat."

"Squawk!"

Petal head (part 1)

I considered Chloe to be a bonafide 'petal head'. A lover of flowers and all of the hippy loving peace crap which came along with it. Her entire existence revolved around flowers, feathers, and love.

Dandelions in particular.

Not roses.

Not carnations.

Not daffodils.

Nope.

For Chloe it was a damn weed.

'As if I should have been surprised by yet, another one of her notorious kooky ideas.'

"What makes a dandelion so special, huh, Chloe? Enlighten me," I asked as we leaned against a rusted chain link fence that surrounded the front of a recently abandoned crack house.

The front yard was overgrown with dandelions and who knows what else. Dirty needles? Used condoms? Empty liquor bottles? Beer cans? Crack pipes? Baggies? Old clothes? Soiled underpants? The possibilities were endless.

Rummaging through that nasty yard would be like a treasure hunt for desperate addicts. Imagine a discovered used baggie of drugs. One could still get a tiny buzz with a lick of the finger, a quick rub inside the baggie to retrieve any granules left behind, then into the mouth the finger went. Instant micro-high. Thankfully, I was not that desperate that day.

Chloe turned and looked at me like an innocent child does towards their loving parent. "People always see dandelions as ugly weeds. Useless, you know."

"They're right," I said. I lit a cigarette and took a heavy drag.

She grabbed my left shoulder. "It's just not true what they say about them, Bug. It's just not true."

I responded with another deep drag off my cigarette and three perfectly blown smoke rings.

"The world sprays poison junk to try and kill them, but they don't know, Bug. They don't know," she whined.

"Who in this theory of yours doesn't know?"

"People, Bug."

"What don't these", I sarcastically used air-quotations, *'people'* know about how special dandelions are to the world, Chloe? Why are you the only one with this," I then leaned in and whispered, "*secret information?*"

She pushed me away. "Stop it. I'm serious."

I replied with more smoke rings. "I can see that."

"Dandelions are just like us, Bug."

I palmed my forehead in utter disbelief and wondered '*How are two drugged out whores like a weed?*'

I could hardly wait for Chloe's explanation, despite the risk of a migraine. "I ain't like no damn dandelion. Besides, a few weeks ago you said we were like feathers or some crap, floating here and there free. So, which is it, Chloe? Are we weeds or feathers?"

Chloe immediately sulked with hurt feelings.

I reached out and took hold of her right hand. "I'm sorry, Chloe. I'm listening. Go on. Tell me about dandelions and the people. I'm listening."

She stared at me.

"I promise. All ears. Right here. Continue."

As punishment, Chloe made me wait a whole two minutes before her explanation was provided.

'Theatrical little twit.'

"Dandelions are beautiful and good for the planet, Bug."

I glanced at the overgrown yard. "Where did you hear that load of malarkey from? A documentary on TV in some John's hotel room?" I snickered.

"Stop," she begged.

"In case you haven't noticed, we're whores and whores aren't beautiful. We're disgusting. They're disgusting."

She shook her head side to side. "Not true."

I countered, "You and I. Disssss…gussssss…tiiiiiiiing. Dandelions, same thing. Disssss…gussssss…tiiiiiiiing"

Chole tried to cover my mouth with her hand. "Shut up. Don't say that. It's not true." She forced my head towards the weeded yard. "Look at them."

I jerked her hand away from my mouth. "Not seeing it, kid. Sorry."

"You're not looking hard enough, Bug. Look harder."

I squinted my eyes. I appeared more constipated than intrigued. "Sorry, still don't see what you do."

"Dandelions have so much good to offer to the world, Bug. Most people can't see their beauty or their goodness because bad people have convinced them they are worthless with nothing to offer. And it's not true. It's just not." She slammed her palms hard against the rusted fence. It rattled loudly and violently shook.

"Careful or you'll get tetanus."

"What's that?" she asked. I often forgot how young and uneducated she was.

"Nothing. Just be careful with the rusted fence. I don't feel like spending the day in the ER."

I wondered, with Chloe's strong insistence about the dandelions, '… *was Chloe really talking about the flower or herself for once?*'

"All I see are ugly weeds that look better than I do right

now."

"You look pretty, Bug."

"You're full of shit."

"I'm not."

"You are. I saw how much cheese you ate last night," I teased. She laughed.

I laughed, too, until she grew serious again.

"Listen, listen," she said, excited while waving her hands all up in my face.

"I'm listening. I'm not deaf, so get your hands out of my face." I smacked them away.

"Dandelions are like us, Bug."

"Let's give this flower talk a rest. What do you say? Let's go get a soda or something." I found I could always distract Chloe with promises of food, drink or *dirt*.

Chloe refused to move from the spot until I saw the dandelions her way. So, I caved and asked, "What do we have in common with a stupid weed, Chloe.? Enlighten me. Please."

She smiled and joyfully replied, "Beauty."

"Beauty? From a weed? *A-hmm.*"

"Exactly! You're getting it. I can tell."

"How can you tell?"

"It's written all over your face."

"Kid, what's written all over my face is a bad hangover not a floral revelation."

'I plan to talk to Tiny about the dirt he's been selling to us lately. Chloe's

been flaking a little too much lately.'

"Nuh-uh."

"Okay. That's it. You've officially lost your damn mind, girl."

"No, I haven't. My mind's expanded. Free. I have chosen to see beauty in all things. You don't. Why?"

"Because I don't want to." I tucked a loose piece of her mousey brown hair behind her left ear. "It's my choice, right?"

"True, but…"

"But nothing."

"But…but…people never see *our* true beauty, Bug. Don't you get it?"

I scoffed, "Our true beauty? You haven't looked in a mirror lately have you, Chloe. We're junky whores. There is nothing beautiful about us. In fact, while we're on topic, I don't want anyone to see the real me. Ever. They haven't in all these years. Why start now? It's all so pointless. And not to mention, a complete buzzkill."

"No, it's not."

"Yes, it is."

"No."

"Yes."

"No. Stop it."

"Why are you so afraid for people to see the real you, Bug? I see the real you."

"You only see what I want you to see."

"I don't believe you."

"I don't care what you believe."

"I think you're beautiful on the inside, Bug." She hugged herself, and then leaned over and squeezed me until I felt as if my bones might break, and we would both lose our balance and fall through the eroded fence.

'Just what I needed. A lockjaw shot. Bad enough I was waiting for a Gonorrhea test result. Courtesy of a John who assaulted me without using protection.'

I shoved Chloe off me. "If you say so, petal head. I don't see any beauty in myself inside or out." I then took a drag off my cigarette and exhaled.

"Bug?" she quietly asked.

I rubbed at my itching nose, "What?"

Chloe stared into my eyes with those doe-shaped brown eyes of hers. I felt the wall I had fought so hard to keep up over the years, buckle.

'Damn your soft eyes, Chloe!'

"I think you're beautiful. Just like that dandelion right there," she pointed her index finger at a flower in the middle of the patch.

"Where?" I asked, as I attempted to follow her finger.

"Right. There."

I had no clue which flower Chole pointed at. I only knew my instincts screamed, *'Cry and hug her!'* But my stone-cold heart said, *'Don't be a wimp!'* So, I gave a simple response with little to no feeling attached, "*Umm*...I see it. It's cute. Thanks."

Chloe ran into the yard and picked the only puffy white dandelion in the bunch. She gleefully ran back and practically shoved it into my mouth.

"What are you doing?" I pushed the puff ball out of my face, only to have it thrusted back in front of my chapped lips.

"Close your eyes, Bug, make a wish and then blow."

I hated closing my eyes and wishing for anything. Especially if birthday candles were involved.

I shoved the puffy flower out of my face again. "My wish is for you to make a wish, Chloe."

"Are you sure?"

"Absolutely. Make your wish for me. I insist."

"Okay. Here goes."

Chloe puckered up her pink lips, closed her eyes and then blew until the fluffy white ball had disappeared and what remained was a naked green stem.

"Know what I wished for?"

"You're not supposed to tell a wish dummy, or it won't come true."

"I wished you would smile more, Bug."

"You just wasted your wish."

"No, I didn't. I have faith one day you'll smile more."

"Never going to happen. Should have wished for something else. Maybe a new tape for your *Walkman*."

I had not believed in wishes for a long time. And smiles were for dreamers. The hard truth: I felt as disgusting on the outside as I did on the inside about myself. Far from beautiful. Repulsive felt more befitting. I wanted so much to hop over that fence and pull every one of those dandelions out of the ground so no more wishes could be made by anyone. Ever.

But I remained stoic, fixated on a sea of yellow topped weeds. I knew what happened to me in the past was not my fault. However, my mind could not and would not allow me to see myself other than repulsive, disgusting and revolting. Three words metaphorically tattooed on my forehead with invisible ink since the age of seven that only creepy men read.

My life was a persistent turnstile of whoring and drugging. Whoring to earn for drugs.

Drugging to forget about the whoring.

I felt sick.

Unclean.

Ruined.

I was conflicted. I hated what I had in common with the dandelions, but I also secretly longed to be a dandelion, just so I could be doused in poison. My existence on this planet could then be all but forgotten. I would finally be free, freer then any of Chloe's feathers.

Chloe's sentimental babble wave had bummed me out. I needed to leave the area.

"Come on petal head. Let's go to the Beans & Jellies Café. Get a drink or something."

Chloe bent over and whispered to a clump of flowers basking in the sunlight, planted next to the sidewalk in front of the dilapidated house, *"Bye baby dandelions."*

I grabbed Chloe by the wrist. "Enough of the flower shit. Come on."

"Okay. Okay."

I snapped back, "Those weren't even baby dandelions. They were Biden daisies."

I turned into my mother in that moment. I did not mean to be so sharp-tongued at Chloe's sensitive nature.

So cold.

So hard.

So cruel.

Unlike my mother, I took no pleasure from cruelty towards, Chloe. I felt remorse but refused to show it. I was stubborn. I was weak.

Chloe turned back towards the flowers. "Sorry I called you the wrong name! Bye, daisies!"

I yanked her arm once more, "Let's go!"

"I'm going. I'm going," she replied with a fresh picked dandelion in her hand.

Petal head (part 2)

Chloe habitually picked wildflowers by the roadside and handed them to random strangers.

"Why, Chloe? Why? Why do you pick flowers for people you don't know? Better yet, why don't you charge them for the flowers?"

She flashed a playful grin. "Because it's beautiful to give to others, Bug."

"That so."

She nodded her head up and down. "Flowers make people smile. I think everyone should smile. Don't you?"

"Not really."

"Here." She handed me a single flower. "Smile."

I grimaced at her gesture and said, "Picking weeds and giving them to strangers isn't beautiful. It's pointless."

"It's not pointless."

"It is."

"I think it shows love and care, Bug. *Sheesh.*"

Deep down, I secretly found Chloe's flower idea endearing. I was jealous of her ability to feel so open and free, despite the horrendous treatment she had endured during her young life.

I could never be like Chloe, even with a sprinkle of envy. I was far too jaded and damaged by others to pick flowers for myself. The world and everyone in it sucked in my opinion.

I often noticed the twisted-up faces people made whenever Chloe approached them with clumps of wilted wildflowers. They acted as if she shoved a sour lemon into their pretentious piehole. Most people avoided any encounters with the homeless on purpose. Even if the encounter included a clump of crappy, wilted flowers, from a hippy chick with a sweet innocent smile.

You know the look I mean. The classic: "*Oh, shit. Quick! Stare down at your phone or something else so the dirty, smelly homeless freak will pass you by and you can then pretend to not feel guilty for being such an ignorant asshole.*"

I wondered, *'Since when had humanity become so damn heartless?'* Then I answered my own question. *'Since I became old enough to see it.'*

I muttered, "Rich bitch," underneath my breath as a twenty-something year old girl pulled out her phone the moment Chloe and I passed her by on the sidewalk.

Chloe attempted to hand her a flower. "Here's a flower I picked specially for you."

The girl instantly recoiled and yelled, "Fuck off trash!"

I sneered at her overreaction and the words of disgust she hurled towards my street sister. She snapped a picture of us to post and mock us online.

"Don't take our picture, you stuck-up bitch!" I shouted in anger. "I'm gonna shove that phone straight up your tight ass!"

She tartly replied, "Why don't you take a shower and get a job loser!" She turned around and walked away.

"Bitch!" I yelled back. Chloe stood by my side, shocked by the interaction which had taken place.

I wondered, '*What if our roles had been reversed? What if life offered me better choices? What if momma chose me over her octopus' boyfriends and whiskey, instead? I could just as easily have been that girl and her me. I'll bet she has no idea how fortunate the cards she got dealt were blessed versus the ones dealt to me, cursed. She didn't struggle with addiction, live on the streets or in smelly shelters where you slept with one eye open to protect your shit and yourself from perverts. She could earn her money the right way. Not on her knees or on her back.*'

Chloe hugged the flower. "It's okay little one. We'll find you a good home."

"*Bet she has no idea how lucky she is,*" I whispered.

"Who's lucky, Bug?"

"No one. Screw her. I'll take your flower."

Chloe smiled, "Really?"

"Yes. Really. And look," I then smiled.

Chloe spun in a circle with her hands towards the sky, "I knew you smiled, Bug. I knew it!"

I playfully shoved her shoulder. "Stop."

It was pointless to compare myself to the snobbish girl. We were in two different worlds with no dramatic change forecasted on the horizon. I decided to erase the argument from my brain.

"Gone!"

"What?" Chloe asked.

"Nothing," I replied. I then gazed downward, and there in the middle of the sidewalk was a lone dandelion flower.

"Look, Chloe, it's a free growing dandelion, just like you."

She turned and gave me a hug. "I love you, Bug!"

"Right back at you, kid," I muttered. Showing my emotions was difficult. "Now get off me. I haven't showered today."

Chloe made a yucky face. "Ewww!"

"I know. I know."

"You might stink on the outside Bug, but the love oozing from within smells sweet."

I rolled my eyes. "Oozing? Really? You're such a weirdo, petal head."

"You love me. I know it."

I never uttered the word *love* to anyone because I never understood what it meant. Therefore, how could I speak or express the word with actions to anyone? I had never been loved by anyone my entire life. At least not in the proper way. Chloe was the only person who loved me in the right way.

I bent down and picked the yellow dandelion flower and tucked it behind Chloe's right ear. "Beautiful," I said, while I moved one of the blue jay feathers from her homemade headband out of the way.

The flower brought back an entertaining memory.

Chloe and I were panhandling by an exit ramp near I75 and Bruce B. Downs Boulevard. Chloe handed a man in a red Porsche a clump of daisies mixed with dandelions she had picked beside the exit ramp. In typical Chloe fashion, she innocently failed to notice the flowers were covered in fire ants.

The driver suddenly yelled out in pain, "You idiot!" before he exited his car and ran around it like he had ants in his pants. Which as it turned out, he did.

In a fit of understandable anger, he chucked the flowers back at Chloe and cursed out, "You dumb bitch!" before he jumped back into his car as the traffic light turned green.

I was left speechless and watched as Chloe nonchalantly brushed bits of flowers and confused ants off her dress.

She smiled at the red car as it sped away and yelled, "Have a groovy day!"

"Unbelievable," I whispered.

"What?"

"You."

"What about me," she asked, confused.

"I would have punched that guy in the dick for throwing ants at me and cussing me out. How can you be so damn nice to people who treat you like shit, Chloe? I don't get it."

"Simple. Compassion."

"Compassion?"

"It was my fault."

"That he acted like a dick to you? I don't think so."

"No. Not that part. I should have checked the flowers before I handed them to him."

"Wait…What?????" My brain was ready to explode.

"And…"

I cut her off. I fumed, "You want me to find him and beat his ass for you?"

She put her hands on my arms to calm me down. "He's a lost soul, Bug. Let him go in peace."

The light bulb of Chloe's logic finally clicked in my brain. "Oh, I get it now. The compassion is for you, not him."

"The compassion is for both of us." She picked a fresh clump of flowers. No ants this time.

"You're too forgiving, Chloe."

"I know. But it's better to love than to…"

"Not loved at all?" I cut in.

"Something like that, yeah. Love feeds peace. Anger robs it."

I shook my head side to side, "Yeah. Yeah."

Chloe approached a white car as it stopped at the intersection. "Some flowers for you."

The woman inside the car took the flowers and smiled.

Chloe turned to me and smiled. She mouthed in silence, "See?"

I just shook my head, bewildered by her resilience. I mouthed back, "No, I don't."

Cooked Cabbage

I met with Tiny and scored *dirt* tapped with a dash of ecstasy. Today was a day of celebration. Chloe's birthday.

"Happy Birthday, kid," I turned to Chloe and said as I paid Tiny.

"It's your birthday, Flowerchild?" He asked.

Chloe handed Tiny a flower. "It is."

"Well, I ain't gonna ask how old you are. I don't need to know that shit."

"She's old enough," I interjected and took the small baggie from his hand.

"Ah-right then," Tiny replied.

"Come on, petal head. Let's party." I waved the baggie before her eyes.

"Groovy."

Chloe and I headed to our secret spot to get high and celebrate her birthday. We also wanted to forget everything and anything about our crappy lives. Our secret spot was an abandoned, rusted out maroon *Ford Taurus* with four flat tires, in a weeded lot surrounded by boarded up, dilapidated buildings. Hidden in plain sight.

Chloe and I fixed up the inside of the wrecked car with fluffy throw pillows, blankets and small plastic plants found when we dumpster dove behind a *Kmart*. I was always blown away by what stores deemed trash.

Chloe always sat in the passenger seat.

Me, I sat on the driver side.

I pulled the small baggie of *dirt* tainted with ecstasy from my back jean shorts pocket. From there, the routine of preparing to shoot up commenced.

Pour heroin powder into a spoon hidden in the glovebox.

Add water from a bottle.

Cook it using a cigarette lighter stolen from a trick.

Once cooked, draw the brown liquid into two needles.

One for me.

One for Chloe.

Tie a shoelace around the upper arm.

Shoelaces were kept from view underneath the front driver seat.

Tap.

Tap.

Tap.

Success.

Veins cooperated for both of us.

Injection.

Lift off!

Injection.

Lift off!

Our journey to freedom from life's pain instantly ensued.

Dirt flowed through my veins like fresh, sweet, tapped syrup bled forth from a maple tree concealed deep in a Vermont forest.

Smooth.

Slow.

Syrupy.

Dirt hugged my innards like the loving arms of a parent. A feeling I never experienced from either of my parents. My mind soon, but only briefly, transformed into memories of my mom.

I quietly whispered, *'I love you mommy.'*

I laid my head back on the car's headrest and welcomed *dirt's* endless cascades of warmth with every fiber of my being. The silence was oh, so, golden until Chloe cheapened its value with her words.

"Man! I would have given anything to have celebrated my birthday in the seventies at Haight-Ashbury, Bug. This is the best birthday present, ever, Bug." She then clutched her heart.

I shot Chloe a side-eye and half-mumbled. "I'm pretty sure Haight-Ashbury was in the sixties, Chloe."

"Sixties. Seventies. Who cares?" She closed her eyes, hugged herself and rocked side to side. "It's all love and it's my birthday today. It's all so beautiful, Bug."

"Love is bullshit," I sourly sneered.

"But I feel it."

"What you feel is the love of Tiny's special birthday blend, petal head. Now hush. You're wrecking my high."

"But it's real, Bug." She then reached over and hugged me tightly. "Can't you feel it?"

"I can't feel anything. But I smell something ripe. You need to put some soap and a razorblade to those hairy armpits, hippie girl. Now shoo! You stink!"

She retracted back to her own seat and said, "You felt the love when I hugged you. I know you did. You can't fool me, Bug."

"Whatever you say. Happy Birthday, kid."

"Thanks, Bug."

Chloe closed her eyes. I, too, closed my eyes and allowed my mind to drift back to the syrupy sweetness of the maple trees and the *dirt* coursing throughout my veins.

'A sweet day to be alive and celebrate… indeed.'

Pricks, Pennies & Pests

I continued my ride in the pickup truck towards North Nebraska Avenue with the blue-collared John. I was headed to meet Chloe, who was probably out front of our main hangout, The Beans & Jellies Café. I was late.

The Beans & Jellies Café was a standard mom and pop coffee house. It had vintage metal farm signs on the walls, mismatched antique tables and chairs. a distressed brown leather couch and a countertop lined with torn red Naugahyde stools. The place resembled a chic shithole. But it served the best damn jelly doughnuts and strongest coffee in the Tampa Bay area.

The owners went by 'Mom and Pop'. They always took care of the working girls. Mom thought of us all as her daughters. Their policy: you never paid for anything if you did not have money. You paid what you could when you could.

"None of my girls go hungry," Mom said, before always handing over a sugary donut and a mug of hot coffee.

Chloe was dressed in an orange sundress, vanilla Go-Go boots, and her outrageous homemade feathered headband. Torn yellow foam-covered headphones from her ancient Walkman hung loosely around her neck and blared inaudible music.

While she waited for me to show up, Clohe hustled folks for money while on their way to the bus stop located in front of the Café.

"Sir?" Chloe asked in her soft, wispy voice, before shoving a grimy used paper coffee cup towards a businessman about to pass her by.

The man sneered at Chloe and dropped one penny into the cup. "Happy now?"

Chloe peered into the cup. She then shouted at the businessman's back, "Peace and love!"

She resumed panhandling.

"Mam? Got anything you can spare?"

Just as the woman dropped two quarters into the cup, Chloe spotted the blue-collared John's pickup truck and screamed out at the top of her lungs, "BUG!"

"CHLOE!" I hollered back. I turned to the blue-collared John. "Hey, man! Stop the truck!"

The jerk braked so hard I nearly smashed my face on the dashboard. Payback I assumed for rejecting his advances during the ride.

I exited the truck, and a wave of relief instantly washed over me. The blue-collared John angrily peeled away from the curb. The once fresh crisp morning air became impaled with the smell of burned rubber.

"Asshole!"

A thirty-something lady walked by Chloe and me with a toddler in tow. Chloe multitasked. She half-hugged me and simultaneously shoved the filthy cup towards the woman's face.

The woman rummaged through her purse.

Plop! Plop!

Fifty cents went into the cup.

"Thanks, Mam!" Chloe then turned to me and whispered in shock, *"Fifty cents, Bug. Out of sight."*

I noticed since the last time I saw her; Chloe had added two more blue jay tail feathers to her headband. I grabbed hold of one of them.

"New?"

Chloe nodded her head. "Found them on the ground over on East Hanna under a tree." She gently moved my hand off the feathers. "Cool, right? I just love the colors."

"Cat attack, is my guess."

She pushed my shoulder and whined, "Stop it, Bug. The bird is okay. He just didn't need these feathers anymore. He grew newer, stronger ones. He is flying," she pointed towards the sky, "Somewhere in the sky."

"He's flying alright, inside some happy cat's belly." I reached forward and rubbed her stomach.

"Shut up," she cried and shoved my hand away.

"Okay. You're right. The little birdy is fine."

Chloe vacillated between a smile and a pout. I sensed she doubted by sincerity regarding the bird's well-being. I also suspected she thought I might be correct about the bird's true fate.

"Where have you been, Bug? It's been days," she grumbled. I knew she needed a fix.

I replied with an indifferent tone to my voice, "Here and there.".

Chloe did not need to know about where I had been, nor the things I had done to earn the money to help support our dependent drug habit.

Chloe nodded her head in the direction of the truck which had just left. "Groovy time?"

I turned towards my left and saw the blue-collar John disappear around the corner at the traffic light down the road aways. I adjusted my shorts in the front. The uncomfortable squirming done during the ride caused them to creep up. Everything below the belt felt numb.

"Better?" she asked with a quizzical look.

"Better."

To someone driving by, it looked as if I had caught a horrific case of college crabs.

I bumped Chloe's hip with mine. "Buy me a coffee and I'll give you *all* the filthy details about him." I nodded in the blue-collar John's direction.

Chloe paused and then shot a suspicious look at me. "Wait a minute."

I stuck out my bottom lip, "What?" I innocently asked.

"You've got money for coffee. You just tricked. You have been doing it for days, right? Or were you locked up?"

I grabbed the filthy cup from Chloe's hand. "I wasn't locked up, petal head. I never get locked up."

"So, why can't you buy your own coffee, then?"

"Because I hardly made shit the last few days. And what I did make…" I trailed off and grinned. "Well, you know…"

Chloe's bottom lip jutted out and her arms crossed. She snapped, "Bug! You promised you wouldn't score without me."

I shrugged my shoulders, "Shit happens."

"That's not fair. I've been going without…"

I cut her off. "Life isn't fair, kid. Thought you knew that by now."

"What about that guy?"

"What guy?" I asked. I played dumb. I knew who she meant.

"The truck guy."

"What about him?"

 Did he stiff you or something?"

"Oh, he stiffed me and something." I almost gagged as my mind re-lived the moment.

"Do you have money for Tiny?"

I raised my eyebrows. "I can hardly afford a cup of coffee."

Chloe grew pissed. I broke a promise we made. Neither of us scored *dirt* without sharing it. I had never kept my end of the bargain. If Chloe knew how many times I got high without her, I would have no family.

I jiggled the cup. Several coins clanked as they ran into one another inside the small space.

"Sounds like enough change for a cup of beans and a jelly doughnut." I gave her my best pity face. "Come on. We can share."

Chloe stared at me in disbelief. She clearly struggled to find a morsel of the peace and love jumbo she thrived on so much.

I got close to her face. "Come on, Chloe. Chloooo-weee! Bug needs her caffeine fix until she can get a…" My index fingers made air quotation marks, *"…real fix for both of us."*

Chloe snatched the cup from my grasp. I felt the little bug legs as they began to scamper about my skin in various places. My countdown clock now officially ticked towards dope sickness soon. I needed to hit the streets and earn or else.

I fidgeted with the semi-fresh track marks on my arms. I then glanced down at the track marks hidden between my toes. My new spot. The veins in my arms were cooked.

I noticed I needed a new pair of shoes. My worn-down flipflops were eroded even though they managed to make my red painted toenails look nice; like a posh penthouse pet thrust in the middle of Skid Row.

Chloe muttered, "I can't talk to you yet."

She put her worn out headphones on for two *Led Zeppelin* songs. I had never seen her so mad over me getting high without her.

I never understood Chloe's rarity to get pissed off over anything. Angry Chloe was as rare as a sighting of the Loch Ness Monster or Big Foot. Even despite her mom's many boyfriends having done her wrong like momma's boyfriends had done me. Chloe's soul should have been destroyed, same as mine and others who lived on the streets. The worst thing the abuse caused was her addiction to drugs. Chloe remained kind, otherwise. A giant mystery, indeed.

I heard the faint sound of Robert Plant belting out, *"When the levee breaks, I'll have no place to stay"* from Chloe's Walkman, when she had finally removed the headphones from her ears.

"How long's it been for you?" she asked. "Don't lie to me. I'll know if you're lying." She stared into my eyes.

I gave my hair a good rustle and looked away. "Too long"

I lied. I was coming down. Chloe knew it, too.

"Liar."

I begged her again, "Please, Chloe? I need caffeine and sugar. Lots of sugar. Just something to get me over until I can get back out there for both of us."

She caved, "Fine," I knew I would win her over with promises of *dirt* in her not-so-distant future.

"You're the best, Petal head!"

"You want to know something, Bug?"

"What," I asked, as I took a hold of the cup.

"You're really living up to your name, today."

"How's that?" I asked.

Chloe playfully pushed me towards The Beans & Jellies Café door. "Bugging me for this. Bugging me for that. A real pest."

I turned around and coyly replied, "And you love me for it", before I planted a kiss on her dirt-smudged cheek.

"Think Pop's got any strawberry jellies today?" she asked.

Another Day, Another...

Being homeless and addicted to heroin was the closest thing to hell on earth in every sense of the word. There was nothing enticing about one second of it. Unless: puking, crapping your pants, losing teeth, sleeping with strangers for money just to score, having a tent to call home *(if you were lucky)*, rare personal hygiene opportunities, dealing with frustrated paramedics trying to save your overdosed ass, but struggling because you have blown out all your veins. And the worst part, never knowing if you would earn enough money in time for your next fix before dope sickness took over.

Being a homeless drug addict was never on my bingo card in life. Hell, either one would not have made it onto my *'bucket list'*.

But things happened or did not happen.

Directions changed.

Roads became bumpier or closed off.

Doors were slammed and sometimes nailed shut.

One was left with but a handful of choices to survive; quit while you were ahead, blend into your pathetic surroundings like a chameleon on a dead plant or fight like an angry alley cat to escape the bag of shit life tossed you into before it twisted that sucker tight and chucked you off the nearest bridge to drown in a nasty river of doom.

I chose the chameleon route.

I lacked survival skills in the beginning. I found it easier to blend in than to stand out. I gave up on life, but not entirely. I did, however, give up any belief in myself. I was weak. But not enough to quit just yet. Though I would be lying if I said the thought never crossed my mind.

Bad thoughts arose in my mind often like that one song on the radio you could never stand hearing. The song you would crawl across the floor bleeding out just to shut the radio off and never hear it again. We all have that one song.

Somehow, someway, no matter how gross life got, *dirt* was always there for me like a warm blanket, an old friend. It wrapped its arms around me and showered me with love. No questions. No judgements.

I felt warm.

I felt loved.

I felt content.

Dirt devoured every negative thought that swirled around inside my head. It embraced my soul. It pieced my broken heart back together with invisible duct tape.

The hurt…gone.

The shame…gone.

The anger…. gone.

The disappointment…gone.

The confusion…gone.

The loneliness…gone.

I eventually learned those were cliched lies I had told myself every time I shot up. Want to know the truly sad part about it all? I actually believed those lies every time I felt the warmth of *dirt's* touch ooze its way from the top of my head all the way down to my half-polished, raggedly looking toenails.

Addiction and homelessness coaxed me into doing things I never imagined I would ever have done for survival. The power of the drug, the power of starvation was overwhelming. I found myself doing or being done to by Johns, vile, unspeakable things. Things worse than what momma's boyfriends had done to me in the back bedroom of our trailer when I was a child. Things I will never utter, not even on my death bed.

As for my dreams of a better life? The dream of becoming something good in the world? *Fuck it.*

Once the streets, once *dirt* consumed me, nightmares became my dreams.

Lather, Rinse, Repeat...

EARLY MORNING:

I woke up under an overpass.

My filthy body sprawled out.

I smelled like a decayed buffet.

And I looked even worse.

The circle of buzzards did not desire a taste of me.

Why would a John?

I was extremely hungover.

I needed a shower and a fix.

No. Wait. A fix and then a shower.

Typical junkie.

Dirt came before anything and everyone.

Always.

It was the first thought I had upon opening my eyes.

And the last thought I had when my eyes closed.

I failed to earn enough to score last night.

I mean, I had earned enough.

But I owed my dealer.

Tiny refused to front me anymore until I paid off my debt.

I had to compromise my craving for drugs with booze.

My head hurt badly.

My stomach yearned to lurch.

But it was too empty.

I had nothing on the inside to throw up.

Except my feelings.

My bladder was upset, too.

The moment I sat up, my bladder felt ready to burst.

I pee-pee danced my way to a gas station.

The bathroom was on the outside.

I needed a key.

A clerk rudely threw the key at me.

Bitch barely missed my eyeball.

I jiggled the lock to the bathroom door.

'Finally!'

The bathroom was dimly lit.

I could not say the same for the mirror.

It was bright and screamed, 'Clowny the Whore' back at me.

I felt like as if I were inside a funhouse at the County Fair.

Only this house, this bathroom was not so fun.

I stared hopelessly back at my pitiful reflection.

"Christ, Bug! You look like shit warmed over."

I looked as bad as I felt.

The porcelain sink had seen better days.

I used it to freshen up.

The pink soap oozed from the dispenser.

It reeked like an old lady's perfume.

I related to the small sink.

Its rusted pipes and chipped top.

Used.

Abused.

Unappreciated.

Despite the numerous services it provided for so many.

Hard brown paper towels chaffed my privates as I dried off.

I checked my bag.

No toothpaste.

No gum.

No money to buy them either.

"Dammit!"

I rinsed my mouth out with what remained of a now flat soda.

I purchased it last night to chase the cheap booze down with.

I fluffed up my greasy, blonde hair with my fingers.

I threw a scowl at my tired reflection.

"Time to go to work, skank-bait."

I turned off the light and opened the door.

The sun immediately delivered a bitch-slap to my pupils.

"Ooh!"

I covered my eyes with both hands like a Vampire.

My head pounded even harder.

I left the key stuck in the door lock and walked out.

"Screw that rude cashier. Let her come fetch the key herself."

Within minutes, I was approached by a trick.

We snuck into a nearby alleyway.

I provided him service with a *gag* - no smile.

I needed to earn more cash to buy *dirt* for Chloe and me.

Plus, a tube of toothpaste for just me.

Dope sickness started to set in hard.

I needed to band-aide the crappy way I felt - ASAP.

I mooched a cup of coffee with extra sugar.

Sugar is, was and will always be a dopers best friend.

A car honked for my attention.

It was a hefty geek who waved me over.

He wore a grease-stained Atari T-shirt circa 1980's.

"Probably still lives with his parents. Brilliant."

The day just kept getting better. *(sarcasm)*

But a hustle was a hustle.

Cash was cash.

"Suck it up, Bug!" I muttered.

I nearly retched climbing into the four-door white car.

The backseat was packed to the ceiling with garbage.

Old magazines, dirty clothes, and fast-food wrappers.

The view from the back window was blocked.

His nasty car made me feel momentarily clean.

One whiff of the inside of the car told me he was a hoarder.

He needed a shower worse than me.

"You've got this, Bug," I whispered.

I repeated those words in my head until it was over.

Victory.

The geek was literally a *'one minuteman'*.

For once I felt the Universe was on my side.

A few more bucks had been earned.

Almost there.

I hid the money inside Chloe's Go-Go Boots.

I had *"borrowed them"* after one of my flipflops gave out.

I planned to steal a new pair next time I went to the store.

Chloe would be pissed I borrowed her boots without asking.

However, all would be forgiven once I gave her some *dirt*.

The geek dropped me off back in front of the Café.

It was not long before another horn honked for me.

East Hollywood Street, here I come.

Or he comes sooner rather than later, hopefully.

LaRue

LaRue was barely eighteen and pregnant by a one-time John who refused to wear a condom when he had raped her. His violent actions were revenge after she rejected his offer for a date. She considered getting rid of it but changed her mind the moment she felt a slight flutter burst forth from a tiny butterfly growing inside her belly.

"I'm going to keep it, Bug," she would tell me, her brown eyes filled with signs of exhaustion. The closer LaRue got to her due date the harder it had become for her to work as many hours as possible on the streets. Extreme summer heat, lack of available food, no comfortable place to sleep, let alone sit and a strong addiction to *dirt* never often hindered LaRue. Despite the many odds against her, somehow, LaRue always managed to soldier ahead and get the job done.

I thought, *It must be motherly instinct. Where a mother automatically protects her child at all costs, including sacrificing her own life.'* I mean, the sentiment from LaRue was there even while using drugs during her pregnancy. Addiction could have cared less about her baby. Heartless bastard.

Momma lacked motherly instinct. I worried sometimes that I might, too, because of genetics. I pondered this as I pressed my hand against LaRue's large ebony stomach. I tried to feel the baby kick. I secretly longed to feel maternal, just not pregnant. I could barely take care of myself, Chloe or a feral cat I fed scraps to. I named him, 'Unlucky'. After me.

I used to dream where momma cared about me. I mean, truly cared. Not because of an obligation. More like genuine, from the heart. A wished all my life before she died for one maternal instinct to shine through. Just one. One where she protected me from the wolves instead of throwing me right into their den. Never happened. Thanks to her lack of love and care, I believed dreams do not come true.

"This baby is going to help me get clean and stay clean, too. It's going to give me a purpose, Bug. You'll see."

"I know it will, LaRue," is what my lips spoke. But my head thought, '*No it's not. Dirt's got you too tight by the tail, tiger. It ain't letting you or any of us go. You've never stopped using dirt since you peed positive on a pregnancy test stick at some seedy gas station.*'

I suddenly looked up at LaRue, excited. "Hey! I felt it kick." I had expected the same excited reaction from her to my experience. Instead, I found her gaze fixed across the street at our dealer, Tiny. I gently patted LaRue's arm.

"I know. I know."

She rested her head upon my shoulder.

LaRue was thrown out of the house at sixteen for getting pregnant by her high school boyfriend. Before her ex-boyfriend arrived on the scene and convinced her sex was the same thing as love and basically ruined her life, LaRue had a bright future in journalism. She was on the right track with good grades and a part-time job at a local newspaper.

Now, the only tracks LaRue traveled on were composed of *dirt,* destination unknown and various unpleasant stops along the way. All it would take to derail her was one bad batch of *dirt.* Everyone on the streets knew the risk of taking drugs. But those same folks also believed *dirt* fixed the hurt. So, it was worth the risk.

'Lies!'

LaRue had lost her first baby two months into the pregnancy. Her boyfriend dumped her after the unfortunate tragedy struck. She was devastated and unable to function until someone on the streets introduced her to *dirt.* While her ex-boyfriend caught footballs on a college scholarship, LaRue caught STD's, missed their lost baby, and struggled daily to function. *Dirt* became the only thing which cradled the loss and pain LaRue felt on the inside.

LaRue's stomach and feet were so swollen. I helplessly watched as she waddled over to the passenger side of a car which had pulled up looking for a date. LaRue's royal blue mini dress clung to every nook and cranny on her body.

I waved in her direction and mouthed, *"be careful,"* as the car pulled away from the broken curb.

LaRue waved back and mouthed, *"I will."*

Every day LaRue promised herself she would get clean and be there for her baby. Yet, every day she remained *dirty* until the tragic end of her life arrived…exactly three months after the birth of her son, Trey.

"Sorry, Tiger."

Paula

The corner of my eye caught Paula; a twenty-five *(who resembled more of a thirty-five-year-old)* 5'2" spitfire, with brown hair styled in two low-hung ponytails. She crossed the street to the other side without a care of on-coming traffic.

I screamed, "Lookout, Paula!" just as a maroon four-door car slammed on its brakes.

The driver laid down hard on the horn and yelled, "WATCH IT, WHORE!!"

"SCREW YOU!!" Paula retaliated and continued her strut as if nothing had happened.

Typical Paula. She never looked back. Literally or physically. She cared less about the guy who almost hit her with his car. The shocked bystanders stood with adrenaline pulsating through their veins. No one. Paula lived in her own freaky world. Paula lived by one rule; *Keep on moving. Never look back. Ever.* She practiced what she preached, too.

Paula tipped her head back and shouted out towards the sky as loud as possible, *"Boogie fever! Boogie down!"*

I shook my head and thought, *'High as fuck.'*

Paula donned a pair of red tracksuit pants with double-white stripes that ran vertically down the sides and a semi-dirty white tank top. A headband with two giant Styrofoam balls covered in red glitter and attached to long springs, bounced about on the top of her head.

"Probably boosted that stupid thing from a Dollar Store," I mumbled.

Paula hollered from across the street, "Hey, Bug!"

"Hey, Paula!" I shot back.

"I got the boogie fever, Bug!"

Paula then danced to fit her wild personality.

No shit. (eyeroll)

"I noticed," I replied.

Paula was known on the streets to be hopped up on speed almost 24/7. She had no choice. Without uppers, Paula fell very low into the dumps. Paula's mood could plumet far enough where she has been talked off the ledges of several buildings in the Tampa Bay area by her street family and sometimes the police. Paula hated when cops got involved because it meant she would be put on a 51/50 hold. With her street family, she was guaranteed more speed to remedy the dire situation.

"Next stop – crazy town!" she routinely shouted out before the squad car door slammed shut and her voice was silenced for the next seventy-two hours.

Any time spent with Paula rivaled a circus loaded with insane clowns. One could never predict which way the pendulum of insanity would swing until they were under the metaphoric tent with Paula… *(aka: hanging out with her)*.

Paula's speed-fueled ventures literally had her talk, walk, and eat at a mile a minute. To try and edge a word into a conversation with her was simply impossible. And half the time, not worth the effort. Paula never heard your voice over the sound of her own, or perhaps the voices that chatted inside her head. If Paula's blood were ever to be tested it would be made of sugar, caffeine, speed, and one giant pinch of bullshit.

What rolled across Paula's tongue and poured out of her mouth was mainly nonsense. No one knew Paula's true story. Then again, no one really knew anyone's truth on the streets. People usually shared their version of the truth. Paula was no different. Except her stories typically exceeded the exaggeration bar.

Paula habitually lied. One time she claimed to come from a royal bloodline. Another, she was an orphan. And still another time, she was once a popular singer in a rock band who willingly gave up fame and fortune for life on the streets.

'I think she and Chloe might be related.'

No one understood why Paula turned lying into such an artform. Maybe the lies made her feel important and not so insignificant to the world. Insignificance was a feeling most homeless addicts were well acquainted with.

If Paula got caught in a lie, she claimed not to care what that person thought. Yet, more lies to cover a lie. She cared but would continue to spin lies faster than Rumpelstiltskin spun gold, until whoever the person she spoke with caved and let Paula's truth prevail. Even if it was still a lie.

"Who are they anyway? And why should I care what they think of me. Fuck 'em!" Paula said.

People on the streets drifted in and around Nebraska Avenue and its many side streets. Many for drug overdoses, some returned home, others were rescued from their pimps or traffickers by cops, street families broke up, some opted out of life, and others were in jail or rotting in prison in a 6' x 6' cell. And still many arrived fresh off the bus hoping for a better life in the Sunshine State. The influx never stopped. It merely rotated like a pig on a spit to avoid the burn.

The harsh reality? People on the streets were treading water in their individual cesspools of agony and torment. They had to decide to fight or drown. To fake as if all was right in their world, when it was not or face reality. Many were so preoccupied with keeping their head above water, they failed to notice those drowning right beside them. All of us were locked up in an indefinite self-preservation mode cycle.

Paula screamed out my name again from across the street, "Check it out, Bug!" She tilted her head forward and made those red-glittery head bopper things dance on top of her head.

"Gotta boogie on now, girl."

I called back, "Boogie on then, girl! Catch you another time."
I waved her on.

"Thank God she split! I don't have the energy for that girl today."

Paula eased down the sidewalk like one of those speed walking exercise soccer moms inside the *University Shopping Mall* until she transformed into a red speck far off in the distance.

I was relieved once Paula had disappeared entirely from my view.

'Boogie down!'

Back to My Day

I am once again alone on the streets.

Purple tank top.

Cut-off jean shorts.

Chloe's vanilla-colored boots.

On the prowl for money.

A cute Wallstreet knockoff looking guy wanted a quickie.

The money pot was growing.

If this pace kept up, the pot would soon be traded for *dirt*.

NOON:

"Shit!"

The sun disappeared.

Out came the gray clouds.

It suddenly poured down rain.

I got soaked.

Florida and their damn spontaneous rain showers.

"Gee, thanks."

How I wished for a bar of soap.

It was a free shower from Mother Nature.

Might as well take advantage of the gift, right?

The rain should have made me cleaner.

But I felt far from clean.

No amount of rain could wash off the filth that covered me.

Inside or out.

Harder rain pelted downward.

Regardless, I continued to hustle until I no longer could.

No choice.

I needed *dirt* soon or else.

Cars continued to woosh on by.

The rain a worse turn off than my hygiene habits.

"Shit!"

Not one taker willing to risk it.

The rain cascaded even harder.

Business had officially halted.

"Damnit! I can't catch a break!"

Johns did not want rain-soaked whores in their car.

'Selfish jerks!'

EARLY AFTERNOON:

I huddled underneath a faded-white eve behind a store.

My dope sickness, stronger.

I needed candy to curb the craving.

I reached into Chloe's left boot.

A bag of shoplifted gummy worms successfully retrieved.

I ate the entire bag.

The entire bag.

My first meal of the day.

The strong jolt of sugar helped.

But not enough.

I still felt dope sick.

My toes hurt.

Chloe's boots were a size too small for my big feet.

I sat down on the semi-wet pavement.

I hugged my scabbed knees tightly.

I struggled to stay dry underneath the tiny white eve.

I felt like a smelly swamp turtle smushed inside its shell.

I needed a shower, badly.

I mean, badly.

The wind kicked up.

I was cold.

I was soaked.

And the tiny eve failed to protect me from additional wetness.

I was not surprised by it.

Life never offered me protection.

Protection was a foreign experience to me.

My dad never protected me.

Momma never protected me.

Momma's boyfriend's sure as hell never protected me.

They always took advantage of me.

God never…

You know what?

Never mind.

God never loved me.

I never loved myself.

I hated myself.

Oh, how I despised dope sickness.

The days just sucked overall.

I wanted to quit.

Everything.

Right then.

Right there.

Dirt.

Hustling.

Life.

All of it.

Just one wrong batch of dope.

Just a little bit more in the needle than usual.

Bam!

Over.

But I lacked the courage and strength to follow through.

And even if I pulled the plug, I still had nowhere to go.

A potter's field maybe.

If they would have me.

But only if someone cared enough to acknowledge me.

The truth?

No one cared about me.

I was a drugged-out whore.

A life loser.

Maybe my street sister, Chloe, cared about me.

But who knew how long she would stick around.

We were both homeless junkies.

If I died, Heaven would say, "No thanks."

Hell would say, "Piss off."

I suppose I literally had nowhere to go.

On earth.

Or in the unknown.

Confusion washed over me in powerful waves.

Finally, the rain began to lighten to a drizzle.

I stared at the wet pavement.

My heart felt heavy.

I knew I could not abandon the streets.

I intently gazed at the track marks on my skin.

The marks soon merged into blurred lines.

It was then I had an epiphany.

"My life's been just one pathetic. giant blur."

The only thing I saw clearly…

I could not bring myself to ever abandon *dirt*.

I was too addicted.

Years of abuse and homelessness had convinced me of such.

Told me *dirt* had my back.

The streets were there for me when no one else ever was.

How could I go on without either of them?

The answer?

I couldn't.

I started to cry.

I thought about my dad.

My heart existed vacant.

Nevertheless, anger moved in.

I shouted, "Rot in hell, Asshole!"

I then thought about momma.

I mumbled to myself, "Drunk bitch! I was there for you! I cleaned up your piss and shit! Your vomit! I held your hand as you took your last breath. All you ever cared about were your boyfriends. Loaded and laid was the motto you lived by until the very end. You never cared about what happened to me. Never! I hate you! Fuck your precious Jack, too!"

Her octopus tentacle-handed testicle-driven boyfriends' came to mind.

Different sizes.

Varied shapes.

Some clean.

Some unkempt.

All putrid in appearance, regardless.

Their grubby hands.

Their contrast sized penises.

Both encompassed my childhood like horny villagers with tiki torches and pitchforks.

Each parked at the helm of my innocence.

All fueled by my fear.

Every one of them driven to action by the devil himself.

I thought of the endless parade of Johns trapesing in and out of my body parts like a 24-hour convenience store.

'Always convenient for them. Forever inconvenient for me.'

I grabbed handfuls of my shaggy bleached hair.

I shook my head side to side.

I screamed, "*Aaaaaaaaaaaaaaaaaaaaaaaaa! Sick bastards!*"

A spark of fire erupted down inside.

The glow evolved into a flashover within seconds.

My insides burned.

My soul was torched.

My heart black as coal.

All that was within me now charred.

Rage consumed me further.

I stood up.

Then I repeatedly punched the white cinder block wall behind me.

"Fuck you! Fuck you! Fuck every one of you!" I yelled.

The mental, emotional, and physical pain released.

It was all too real.

Too overwhelming to contain.

The rage eventually brewed down to a simmer.

While the physical pain from hitting the wall set in.

I stared down my bloodied hand.

My knuckles tender to the touch.

I winced and scolded myself.

"Why'd you go and do that to yourself, Bug? Dammit!"

I needed some ibuprofen and bandages.

This meant less money for *dirt*.

And extra time on the streets to earn that money back.

"Shit!"

I fell against the same wall I punched the crap out of.

To my surprise, the wall did not punch me back.

It did not reject me.

It did not shove me off of it.

It did not try to fondle me.

Unlike people, the wall was not cold, cruel, or uncaring.

No.

The wall simply caught me as I fell.

It cradled me like a loving parent.

It gently guided my broken soul to the ground.

I was surprised by its kindness.

By its unyielding care.

It appeared to ask nothing of me.

It was just there.

For me.

Alone.

How I longed to be held with such unyielding care my whole life.

I curled up into a ball and cried.

I cried until I puked up the gummy worms and stale soda.

My sugar rush to stave off the cravings for *dirt* – vanished.

I was dope sick more than ever.

My head hurt badly.

My stomach officially emptied.

My heart, destroyed.

LATE AFTERNOON:

I remained up against that wall until the rain stopped.

I thought, *'Time to pull your shit together, girl!'*

I dried what tears remained.

I wiped the puke crumbs from the corners of my mouth.

I dipped my bloodied knuckles in a puddle of dirty water.

I then entered a gas station store where I stole a packet of ibuprofen, band aides and some gum.

I was getting too dope sick to spend what money I had earned thus far.

Time to hit the streets, again.

Business immediately picked back up where it had left off.

I winced with each trick for the remainder of the day.

I was too sober.

I was too dope sick.

I felt all of it.

And needed to feel none of it.

What I needed was a fix… soon.

The ibuprofen failed to stop my hand pain.

Just one more trick and I earned enough to visit Tiny.

I finally landed one.

A regular.

A fast one.

Bonus.

The dope sickness had grown stronger, and I was weaker.

It felt like tiny little bugs were crawling underneath my skin.

Ten minutes later, I met up with my dealer, Tiny.

Waves of relief were washing over my body while holding that small bag of powdered paradise in my hand.

Knowing all the emotional and physical pain I carried with me, like ghosts trapped inside a haunted vessel, would soon vanish back into their secret crevices.

At least for a while, anyway.

I had not seen Chloe, so I decided to use it all for myself.

'Next time, Sis. I promise. I even took good care of your boots. See? No puke or bloodstains on them.'

I found a grassy noll out of the public view and sat down.

Lighter.

Check.

Spoon.

Check.

Water bottle.

Check.

Shoestring.

Check.

I cooked it and shot up.

I then lay back on the soft grass and watched the sky morph from reddish orange to eventually black.

The sun had finally set on yet, another horrid day.

I had survived it all.

All thanks to *dirt* and that kind white cinder block wall.

Beautiful wall.

Loving wall.

My wall.

The moon would soon arise.

So, too, would I.

Eventually…I got really wasted.

I closed my eyes and placed my arms horizontally in the grass as if I were an airplane prepared for takeoff. The *dirt* had delicately merged together with my pain and blood which coursed within my weak veins, like a rampant mudslide. All of my bad memories instantaneously vanished into a sea of murkiness.

How I wished that feeling would last forever.

I knew it would not.

But I still wished for it anyway.

Seeing Stars, Baby

I stood out in front of a combination gas station and convenience store. My small boobs were on low-key display courtesy of a yellow tube top I borrowed from big-chested Paula. I had to pull the top up every few seconds or risk being arrested for indecent exposure. I paired it with white shorts cut so high; you could have seen my panties…if I wore any.

The shorts used to be ripped up jeans I found at a clothing donation box in a parking lot. Someone failed to shove them all the way inside the container. Based on their condition and style, they sure had themselves one hell of a time in the 80's.

I borrowed a pair of scissors from Pop at the Beans & Jellies Café and trimmed them up. The only trouble was, I failed to follow the old rule; measure twice, cut once. So, the shorts came out shorter than I had intended. *Oops!* It turned out my mistake mattered not. It was better for business. Johns loved shorty shorts. The shorter, the better.

Once again, I found myself in need of cash to score *dirt*. No surprise.

Typical cycle of a junkie's life…

Earn the money.

Buy the dope.

Get high.

Earn the money.

Buy the dope.

Get high.

This *'hamster stuck on the wheel going nowhere pattern'* had to occur, no matter whether it was rain or shine to avoid the joys of dope sickness. Real fun stuff, too.

Runny nose.

Tingling vibrations when peeing.

Cold sweats.

Nausea.

Vomiting.

Body aches.

Diarrhea.

Depression.

Anxiety.

The sensation of bugs crawling all over your skin.

Feeling like your bones were injected with battery acid.

There were other reasons, too.

For me personally, *dirt* equaled avoidance.

Avoidance of emotional pain.

Avoidance of mental pain.

Avoidance of physical pain.

Avoidance was standard addict behavior 101. And I was an A+ honor roll student in the class. I believed if I kept it up, I would soon be crowned valedictorian of the streets.

Each avoidance appeared like a deep root attached to an olive tree who only bore forth rotten fruit. In my mind, it was easier to bury sullied pits inside the *dirt* for continued life, than to throw them in the trash and heal from the pain.

'If healing from my past was even a remote possibility,' I often thought.

I had no clue if I could or would ever heal.

I had no clue if I even wanted to heal.

Avoidance had become so easy.

Too easy, in fact.

It never mattered how disgusted I felt being touched by Johns, if I had poor hygiene, if I were dope sick or if I was in the midst of a mental health breakdown. I had to earn money for my habit or deal with my demons and horrendous withdrawals simultaneously.

I must therefore earn or experience the burn.

My options were none.

Nighttime was usually the best time to earn money. Although early morning was good, too. Both times had many horny men on their way home from a hard day's work or on their way to a hard day's work.

Countless men starved for affection and appreciation before getting neutered by grumpy bosses, wifey tailored honey-do-lists, daddy duties and more. I assumed their fruit trees which bore forth stiff bananas and wrinkled berries were just as rotten as that olive tree of mine.

I blocked out any guilt that attempted to creep in like a thief bent on awakening my conscience. Me, have compassion for their significant others or family; screw that. What I had been through. The hell I had endured which resulted in a life on the streets. Unloved. Plus, my need for a fix outweighed any morals, character, values, or integrity.

What I wanted is what mattered the most.

'To hell with their perfect white picket fence lives!'

The tables were turned in my favor.

My control.

I was on top of the world.

If it were upside down, that is.

Being upside down meant I was actually at the bottom of the ocean. Lower than a pile of whale shit.

Top of the world.

Hardly.

But I lied to myself that I was anyway.

I readjusted Paula's overstretched yellow tube top before my eyes got mesmerized by a blinking yellow traffic light perched across the street.

Light.

Dark.

Light.

Dark.

Light.

Dark.

The flashing light reminded me of a city firefly.

I remained fixated on that lone yellow traffic light and longed for the days when momma and I used to lay on our backs in the field at night and watch the fireflies twinkling.

Such simple times.

Happy times.

But those times died long before momma ever did.

Blinking lights, no matter what the source, bred soul aching memories bathed in sorrow, agony, anger, unforgiveness and regret. But they also conjured up longing, love and feelings that made me miss her sorry drunk ass. The result of both situations had evolved into a combination of euphoric anguish only a roll in *dirt* could understand, like a pig to a puddle of cool mud when it got too hot to shoulder any longer.

I thought, *The prodigal daughter has yet to come out of the hog pen and return home at this point in her life. More slop please. Just keep it* coming. *Nothing but crumbs and decayed scraps from the table will be acceptable and welcomed.'*

In my distorted mind, *dirt* developed into straggly arms that hugged me tight while I cried over what could have…no, what my life should have been.

It was a gentle hand that caressed my face and wiped away salty tears. *Dirt* whispered into my ear during dire moments, *"It's going to be alright. Let me in. Trust me."*

Part of me suspected *dirt* was a liar and deceiver like the many men I had encountered before becoming a whore and after. It really was no different than anyone who ventured into my life. Yet, it had such a strong hold on me. An ability to make me see what I wanted to see. To hear what I wanted to hear. To believe what I wanted to believe. To my deceptive heart and mind, *dirt* represented how my momma should have been towards me, but rarely ever was. It was also the many words my momma should have spoken to me but never uttered.

I was far from okay since the day my purity was stolen from me. The men from my past robbed me of my innocence like a callous purse snatcher on the streets. Just took it right from my firm grasp without permission.

My knees were spread apart like a golden clasp. Their wild, unruly, fondling hands rifled their way through my many pockets and folds, over and over in search of pleasure. I would be thrown to the side like trash, only to be snatched up again by another. I was unzipped and opened up, night after night. Rifled through until I was too sore to take being touched anymore. My fabric worn and torn almost beyond repair. But that never stopped them from opening me up in the hopes of more treasure. Despite that, all that remained of me was a handful of purse dirt.

Terrified.

Sick to my stomach.

I constantly fought back.

Always.

I kicked.

I screamed.

I begged.

I even vomited on some of them.

Other times I just laid there, stiller than pond water and begged for it to just be over. None of the past mattered now. It was done. The purse, my innocence had been thrown in a dumpster long ago. Nothing I could do about it.

I was aware that *dirt* fibbed to me on the regular. Plot twist. I too, lied to *dirt*. I pretended each fix cured everything wrong in my life. It did not. The truth: *dirt* was just a short-term distraction. A mere avoidance to my unpleasant past, my disgusting present and disappointing future.

I remained enthralled by the blinking yellow light like a cat drawn to a red laser beam, when a deep, chain-smoking tinged voice broke my stare.

"Hey, baby girl. Do you like to party?" the man asked before taking a deep drag off a cigarette. "Name's, Pete."

I sized Pete up straight away.

'Around forty-five. Confirmed bachelor. Committed alcoholic.'

The noticeable, deep crow's feet perched next to each eye gave his true history. Too much smoking and drinking had clearly taken their toll on Pete's outside. I shuddered to think of his insides. I was certain his liver would survive without issue stuffed inside a mason jar. No need for any alcohol-based preservative.

"Just like Momma's," I whispered. *"His and hers pickled white-trash pâté. A perfect match."*

I saw Pete at the Beans & Jellies Café. We never actually spoke. He worked in construction. Sometimes his crew stopped in for coffee on their way to work. Pop's coffee had a reputation for curing vile hangovers. And Pete undoubtedly loved his nightly beer.

A very unshaven Pete stood before me in a pair of tight blue jeans and a white T shirt. He had a six pack of beer nestled tightly under his left arm. By the look of his bloodshot green eyes, Pete was already two hours into his own party.

"Can I have one?" I asked, as I nodded at the six-pack.

"Well, that all depends, darlin'," he replied.

I played dumb and twirled my hair. "Depends on what?"

Pete eyed me up and down like a porterhouse steak. I shivered at his stare, not sizzled.

"What you gonna give old Pete in return?" He then licked his lips. "Do you like to party?"

I instinctively revolted at the thought of sleeping with him. But, I had a habit that needed to be fed. So, I forced my typical 'hooker smile', adjusted my top and asked, "What did you have in mind, Pete?"

Pete dug a wad of money from his front jean pocket and waved it before my hungry eyes. He raised his left eyebrow.

"How does partying with Pete under the stars sound to you?"

"Okay. Sure." I looked around. "You got a truck or something?"

"What's your name, darlin'?" Pete then leaned in and sniffed my dirty neck. He gave it a quick lick. "Hmm…salty. Too bad old Pete doesn't have some Tequila for body shots." He winked.

I wanted to vomit. I gently eased him off my neck to nail down the negotiations.

"Ease up. No freebies. And my name doesn't matter."

"Well, it does to, Pete. Come on, darlin'. Pete's your friend, right?" He once again waved that thick wad of cash before my desperate, drug starved eyes.

I caved. "They call me, Bug."

"Bug, huh? What, like one of those black widow spiders or something?" He then poked my right ribcage with his index finger in a teasing manner. "Or are you a furry little caterpillar, instead? Hmm?" He reached out to grab my crotch.

I successfully stepped backwards, and he missed.

Like I haven't heard that stupid joke a hundred times.'

"Fuzzy everywhere, I'll bet." He licked his lips again.

"It's just, Bug. No meaning behind it. Okay?" I snapped back.

Pete leaned in and whispered into my ear, *"Do you like seeing stars, Bug?"*

"Who doesn't?"

Pete grabbed a beer from the six pack and offered it to me. I reached for it. But just before I could grab it, he pulled it out of range.

"*Eh. Eh. Eh.* Not so fast. Hold on just one second my fuzzy little caterpillar."

I immediately thought, '*Stop calling me that asshole!*'

He eyed me up and down. "The way I see it, ol' Pete's offered you a beer and the stars. Romance." He took a chug of beer.

'Dirt's the goal, Bug. Just swallow your vomit, flirt with this loser and so you can get the cash.'

I took a deep swallow and cooed out to him, "Bug will give Pete the stars and anything else he wants. How about we start with Pete handing Bug a beer."

"Well, ah' right then."

I swear, I never chugged a beer down so fast in my life.

Pete and I made our way behind the convenience store. He did not want to use his truck. Said the wife might smell me. We drank for a bit and set the empty beer bottles on top of an A/C unit behind the store. Pete left at one point to buy another six-pack. We wound up chugging a twelve-pack between us.

Once the beer disappeared, it was not long before Pete worked up the nerve and mashed me up against the outside back wall of the store. He kissed and licked my neck aggressively.

'Gross! Just gross. Just stop already. Let's get this over with.'

Pete attempted to kiss me on the mouth numerous times. Each time, I turned my head away and protested, "No mouth kissing."

"Alright. Alright. Take it easy baby." He resumed kissing on my neck. "Ol' Pete's kisses feel good, don't they?"

"Yeah, sure. Whatever."

Apparently, my sarcasm mixed with my obvious desire to not screw Pete did not bode well with his ego. The next thing I knew, Pete slammed me incredibly hard against the building's blue cinderblock wall. I knew Pete was going to beat my ass. I was in real trouble. I could have screamed for help, but no one pays any mind to a whore in danger. All I could do was try and stroke his bruised ego and hope for the best.

"They feel good, don't they? Say it, whore!"

"What, they?" I asked, a slight tremble to my voice. I feared saying to wrong thing.

"Pete's kisses." He slammed me again and demanded, "Say it!"

I nodded my head up and down and almost in a whisper replied, "Yes. Yes. They feel good. Pete's kisses feel good."

Pete pulled back from me and stared dead into my eyes. I watched his green eyes instantly morph into jet black. His face grew contorted. He was no longer the surly, redneck I had initially engaged with.

'I'm so fucked! Help!'

"Liar! Say it again and you better mean it or else," he hissed, as I got slammed up against the wall again. He unbuttoned my shorts with such force, they almost tore. He kissed me on the mouth and let go. "I want to hear you say it!"

"Pete's kisses feel good. They feel good. Take it easy, baby."

But it was too late. Pete's anger over my rejection erupted. There was no amount of water to extinguish the fire I inadvertently started with my smart-mouthed attitude. I knew in that moment I was in deep shit.

Pete grabbed me hard by the throat and choked me. All the while his other hand ventured south, down inside my shorts. My metaphoric purse clasp flipped apart so callously. His hands were rough. He hurt me on purpose with each touch, jab and penetration.

"You are going to love the way this makes you feel darlin'. Ol' Pete's going to have you seeing stars. Right?"

I said nothing. I could not respond with his other hand around my throat.

He slammed me up against the wall, "Answer me, whore!"

I barely managed to utter, *"Rrrrrrrright."*

I attempted to pry Pete's tight hands from around my throat. I could barely breathe. I felt faint. He was too strong for me. Nothing Pete did felt good, around my neck or inside my shorts.

I knew death was certain if I did not act fast. I had to get his hand off my neck. I brought my right knee upwards and kicked Pete square in his balls. He released a cry worse than that of a mother at her child's funeral.

"I don't do that Ted Bundy, psycho shit," I yelled out and pushed him off me. "Asshole!" He stumbled backwards and clutched his aching balls.

Pete continued to rub his crotch and winced in horrible pain with each fractioned move. I delivered a solid kick. I felt proud. But my pride did not last for long. Once the impact of my attack on his family jewels subsided, Pete lunged at my throat with vengeance.

"You ungrateful bitch! You said you wanted to see the stars. Well, ol' Pete's gonna make damn sure you see those stars now whore!"

He tightened his grip around my throat even more. Both hands this time.

I panicked and between gasps of air stammered out, "Stop it! Stop it. You're hurting me. Let go of me!"

Pete forced a kiss upon my mouth. I then kicked him in the shin, and he released his grasp. I managed to push him backwards once again, only harder. And because Pete was so drunk, he lost his balance and fell to the ground.

I stood over him and yelled, "We're done here. Keep your money. Sick asshole!"

I turned to leave. Pete reached out, grabbed me by my right calf and yanked me to the ground beside him. He then rolled on top of me and landed several hard slaps across my face.

He bellowed out, "Where do you think you're going, you worthless whore! I ain't done with you! You gotta see the stars ol' Pete's made specially for you."

I kicked and flailed my arms wildly. I tried to strike him anywhere I could. He was too powerful. I lost what little control I had in the situation.

Pete grabbed me by my hair with one hand and proceeded to beat me to a bloody pulp with the other in the form of a fist and alternated open hand. Punch. Punch. Slap. Slap. Punch. Punch. When he grew tired of the slaps and punches, he stood to his feet and kicked me repeatedly in the ribs.

As Pete's slaps, punches and kicks reduced my body to a pile of bruises bathed in blood, all I could say to myself inside my head was…

The streets are mean. They don't care anything about you. They punish you for things you never done to anyone in your life. Robbed. Raped. Beat up. Infected. You're invisible to the world. A nobody to everybody. Until somebody needs a warm body to rub against. Then you're anybody they pay you to be. Being somebody for a moment is better than being nobody for a lifetime, I suppose.'

Pete mercifully grew tired of beating on me. I think he feared if he kept going, he would catch a murder charge.

"Ain't no whore worth going to jail over."

He released his grip on my shoulders and allowed my battered body to fall to the ground. I landed on my left side. I felt worse than flattened roadkill. I clutched my abdomen.

I thought Pete was done until he suddenly stood, straddled over top of me. I grew terrified. I was defenseless and badly beaten. He used his right foot to forcibly roll me onto my back. He wanted to ensure I saw his nasty face one final time. And to confirm I was still breathing.

He quickly rifled through the pockets of my bloodied, torn shorts and retrieved his money. He then hit my nose hard with the wad of cash. "Taking this back. Bitch!"

Pete remained towered over me. He was dominant and clearly in control. He relished in overpowering a prostitute. "I got something else for you, whore!"

I feared the end had come for me. I felt devastated I would be unable to tell Chloe, "Goodbye," or have one last moment alone with *dirt*. I closed my eyes and awaited my demise. Then, I felt something cold and hard land on me. Pete had retrieved a penny from his pocket and tossed it onto my exposed, beaten chest.

"You ain't even worth that much," he said, then spit beside my head and walked away.

Pete left me bloodied, bruised, and abandoned behind the convenience store. Just me, along with chirping crickets, the sounds of traffic, twelve empty beer bottles and a shiny penny.

I remained motionless on my back for what felt like an eternity. My eyes barely focused due to the swelling that had started to set in. I stared at the stars. They were far more beautiful than the ones Pete had shown me as he knocked me around. I started to cry. In the stars I noticed the letter J.

'Momma always warned me about those who fake making the letter J.'

I coughed.

I hurt.

I tried to move.

I hurt even worse.

I knew I had to muster the strength to sit up and move or I could die if Pete came back for round number two.

I sat on the pavement, held my aching head, and thought…

'The worst is when the streets go lifeless. You get nothing. That's when sickness sets in. It's the worst fucking feeling in the world. The puking. The chills. The pain. The itching. It's like thousands of tiny bug legs are scurrying underneath your skin. The bugs won't stop terrorizing you until they feel the sensation of dirt coursing through your veins to quiet them once more.'

My tracked-up arms itched terribly. I tried to stand up but fell down a few times from dizziness. Pete had worked me over well.

'Bwah-astard!' I mumbled through swollen lips.

Pete was not the first to beat my ass. And he certainly would not be the last. Unfortunately.

I eventually managed to stumble away from the convenience store parking lot and to a hospital for treatment. Thankfully, Pete never returned.

I told the nurses I fell. They knew I was full of shit but could do nothing about it. I refused to press charges or give up any information. I was treated and released the same night with a handful of aspirin and another notch added to my nightmare belt. Though Pete may not have gotten off with me that night, he certainly got off from being arrested that night because of me.

'How do you like those stars, ol' Pete?'

Alleys Aren't Only for Cats

Light.

Dark.

Light.

Dark.

Light.

Dark.

I noticed a blinking streetlight whose bulb had seen better days because it had begun to short-out.

I eased my way down a dark alleyway to meet up with my dealer, Tiny. I was in desperate need of a fix. And Tiny held the cure for all which ailed me. I had to score *dirt* for Chloe, too.

Tiny was anything but tiny. He stood almost six-foot-five and was covered in tattoos. There were too many to count. I tried on several occasions with no luck. Tiny appeared burly but was a softy to those who knew him.

"Whatchu need tonight, cock," he paused, "roach."

I jumped at the unexpected sound of his deep voice. "You scared the crap out of me, Tiny. Damn. Don't do me like that." I then tried to catch my breath.

"Thought my good looks startled you, baby," he teased. Tiny notoriously flirted with all the whores on Nebraska Avenue.

"Cockroach, huh?" I replied with a quizzical stare.

He laughed. "Yeah, cockroach."

"Why's that?" I countered with my hand on my hip.

"Cuz you be creepin' and crawlin' in the dark like you're on the hunt for somethin'." He proceeded to mimic someone creeping and crawling.

I rummaged through my tattered purse which I had found in a dumpster. I was in search of the money I had earned earlier in the day.

"Shit! Where is it?"

"You lookin' to get dirty tonight, huh?" Tiny asked.

"Hang-on a minute." I grew nervous. *"Ah! Found it!"* For a moment I panicked and feared the money had fallen through some unknown hole inside the purse.

"Tiny's got whatchu need if you've got what Tiny needs." He then waved a small baggie before my eyes which contained my sweet delight. *Dirt.*

I handed the money over to Tiny. He began to count the dollar bills when a strange look suddenly washed over his face. "This ain't enough."

"I know. Business is slow tonight." I forcibly cuddled up to him. "Wanna take the difference out in trade?" I really hated the idea of banging Tiny. It would not be our first time doing so. But I was so desperate to get rid of the dope sickness setting in. Customers screw their dealers all the time. Having sex for drugs was no biggie. I did that for a living. I just found screwing any man for any reason repulsive in general.

Tiny pushed me off. "Nah. You know I ain't down with that nasty shit with you girls no more."

"Since when?" I asked.

"Since I figured what I get doesn't even out."

"Come on, Tiny. Please. I'm begging you. I really need it." I stuck out my bottom lip and tried to play cute like a toddler.

Tiny shook his head side to side, "*Tsk.* Man." He was clearly frustrated on a potential loss of sale, money or not.

The dope sickness grew stronger. I asked, "What can I get from you for what I gave you? It's all I got. Honest. I'm not holding out. And you know I'm good for it. We're friends, right?"

"Friends ain't got nothin' to do with it. It's business. No money. No business. You sure you don't got nothing else on you?" he asked in a tone of skepticism. Tiny was well aware that junkies lied and tried to pull fast ones.

I pondered.

"Well?" He waved the baggie of *dirt* before my eyes. "Talk to me."

I hesitated, before I reached down into my purse and grabbed ahold of something I was hesitant to part with. But desperate times called for desperate measures. And I was pushed almost past the point of basic desperation.

Tiny waved the baggie with his distinct logo pasted on it, a Sloth, before my eyes again. "Sure, you got nothing else? I know you want it, girl. Come on. Whatchu you holding out on? Show Tiny. I know you got somethin'."

I reluctantly handed over a prescription bottle of uppers.

"I swiped this off a customer. I was saving it for Paula. I owe her some money."

Tiny carefully inspected the contents of the bottle before he jammed it firmly into his front jacket pocket. He handed me the baggie of dope.

"Thanks, Tiny!"

"Bounce before I change my mind." He playfully smacked my bottom.

I silently crept my way back out of the alley and onto the street like a feral cat who had just eaten the canary without a single feather of evidence left behind.

Spinning Wheels, Going Nowhere

Light.

Dark.

Light.

Dark.

Light.

Dark.

I sat in the driver's seat of Chloe's and my secret hideaway.
I was entranced by the orange flame of fire that shot forth from
a lime green lighter I repeatedly flicked on and off.

"Hurry up, Petal head," I snapped. My patience was depleted.

The harsh tone of my voice caused Chloe to hesitate with
further movement. To breathe. To even pour forth the powder
I purchased from Tiny onto an old metal spoon that was
balanced upon her knee.

My last high had worn off and I needed a fix, like yesterday. The spoon we used to cook the dope had seen better days. But it got the job done to satisfaction. So, why trade up and steal a shiny new one from the Beans & Jellies Café', right?

Chloe wore a look of suspicion.

"What's wrong?" I asked. I assumed Chloe's paranoia resided from the sized baggie I had purchased from Tiny. It was smaller than usual. But all I could afford. The morning had been less than satisfactory for available Johns.

"You sure this is as good as what we usually get, Bug?"

'I was right. Classic case of baggie paranoia…self-destorya!'

I snatched the small baggie from her hand and snapped back, "I got it from Tiny." I then flipped the baggie over. "See, there's the same decal, right on the bag. It's good. Trust me. Tiny's never done me wrong." I dipped the tip of pinky inside the baggie and sampled the product for her reassurance. "It's good. Prep it." I then tossed the baggie back over where it landed on Chloe's bony lap.

"But it's so little. Are you sure it's enough for both of us? I need to feel out of sight right now, Bug. I really, really do. It's been a bummer of a day."

"It'll be enough. Trust me. Pour."

"This John, well, he…" she started to say.

"Pour, Chloe and you'll forget about that asshole."

She reluctantly shut her mouth and poured the powder onto the spoon.

I was far from being in the mood for chatter. Especially words or phrases centered around nameless, faceless, smelly, uncouth, Johns. Normally I helped Chloe navigate through rough patches. But I felt super selfish at that moment. Entitled. My fix mattered more. It always did. Ask any junkie if I am lying. Fix over friendship. Always.

Besides, no one was immune to rough days. Whether on the streets, in a posh apartment or even inside a gated mansion. If your lungs breathed life, rough days were guaranteed.

I felt terrible having dismissed Chloe's need to vent. But *dirt* took priority. My day had not exactly been a bed of soft roses either. It was a day peppered with countless, viny thorns. Not a single delicate second in the day. I was beyond eager to stave off the withdrawals, along with any unsavory memories from my entire life.

Chloe shifted her left knee. The one which held the spoon and powder upon it. My nerves went on immediate alert. One wrong twitch and the spoon would tip over and there went our small, but powerful dope.

"Careful, Petal head. Or you're going to spill it."

"I won't. I won't."

"Seriously. Be careful, Chloe. I mean it."

"I am, Bug. I am."

The spoon wiggled slightly side to side.

"Careful…" I reiterated, only louder.

I wanted to snatch the spoon off her animated knee. But I refrained from doing so. I knew Chloe was hurting and I did not want her to feel even more 'less than' then she already did.

I grew moody. Chloe knew it, too. She flipped her internal switch from dreary and antsy, back into her standard happy hippie mode. A tactic she used often to avoid arguments.

"You really need to relax more, Bug. Stress is not good for the soul. Breeds negative vibes. Breathe in fresh air and release your negative energy out and up towards the sky on an exhale."

I felt a bit tart at her suggestion. "So, if I get to breathe out all of this," I used air quotes, "negative energy" …

"Right. Right."

"Okay, let's say I do it. Where does the negative energy go?"

Chloe just stared at me in wonder.

I snapped my fingers in front of her zoned-out gaze. "Hello?"

She popped back. "Huh? What?"

"I asked you where the negative crap I breathe out goes. What happens to it?"

Chloe nodded her head up and down a few times. "Right. Right. The wind. It becomes part of the wind."

"So, it doesn't become someone else's negative energy, then? I mean, I did release it so technically it's free to find another, right?" I was totally screwing with her at this point.

"It becomes part of the wind. It's free to just be."

I shook my head. Bewildered by Chloe's illogical reasoning.

"Watch what I do." Chloe then demonstrated. She took one deep inhale, a deep exhale, followed by a blank, continual stare at the stained roof of the car.

I felt the needle on my annoyance meter climb. "My anxiety…"

"Stress," she corrected.

I shot her a look of death. "Whatever."

"Breathe in," Chloe said.

I quickly inhaled, then exhaled.

"Better, right?" she asked.

"Look, kid, my stress, negative whatever you want to call it, will be released once you stop shaking your leg with the spoon on it. You're making me very nervous."

"Just breathe, Bug. It's fine." She smiled big.

"Focus, Chloe. Just focus on what you're doing. Okay?"

"I'm trying, Bug," she whined. "I think I've got the jitters."

"Just breathe," I replied sarcastically.

"I'm coming down. I'm sorry," she pleaded with those puppy dog eyes of hers.

"I am coming down too, so you can't lose what we've got. I don't have the energy right now to earn cash to buy more. Tiny's shit costs."

"I'm sorry, Bug. I'm really trying to hold on."

"I always buy from Tiny. No one else. You do the same. Got it?"

Chloe despised being bossed around by anyone. It's one of the key reasons she ran away from home. Between her mom constantly in her face and her mom's boyfriends always creeping into her bedroom at night, she could not take it anymore. So, she split. She hoped for greener pastures. It was not long before she realized the green grass in the so-called 'greener pastures' was loaded with piles of steaming manure. Step after step Chloe found herself covered in metaphorical crap.

Chloe disengaged from her hippie mode and straight to a smart-mouthed teenager who thought she knew it all. Annoyed by my advice, she sourly replied, "*Yeah. Yeah.* Tiny's stuff. I know. You never stop hounding me about it. Over and over. You sound like my bitch of a mom."

I reached over and grabbed her firmly by the left arm. I was pissed over her ungrateful attitude and insulted by her calling me a parent. Being called a big sister, I could manage. But being a parent no thanks.

I had been careful in my grab to not cause the spoon, now full of sweet, sweet, *dirt,* to spill onto the floorboard by her shocked reaction. She had instinctively grabbed the spoon handle with her free hand.

"I mean it, Chloe. I'm not screwing around. There's a lot of bad junk on the streets right now. Almost everything is laced with Fentanyl. You buy from Tiny, only. Always. Understand?"

Chloe jerked her arm from my grasp and sneered back, "I heard you the first ten-thousand times you've told me since I've known you. I'm not dumb. Geez. *Tiny. Tiny. Tiny.* You sound like my mom. Always bitching. You're starting to ruin my positive vibe, Bug." Hearing her say, 'positive vibe' indicated hippie Chloe had begun to beat back bad attitude Chloe.

"Okay. Okay." I released the hold I had upon her arm and quietly retreated to my seat. "Just trying to keep you safe, kid."

"I know. And I love you for it, Bug. I really do." She then blew an air kiss in my direction.

I playfully ducked. "Missed me."

Those sad eyes of hers glanced my way as she whispered, *"Always do when you disappear from me for days."*

I successfully fought back tears. "I know, kid." I resumed flicking the lighter off and on. "But I gotta do stuff sometimes without you around, ya know, so I can keep getting you the good stuff."

She replied in a somber tone, "Yeah, I know."

I stuck a syringe into a bottle of water hidden underneath the driver's seat, added the water onto the spoon and mixed it in with the powdered *dirt.*

Chloe remained jerky. Both physically and verbally. The spoon somehow miraculously stayed on top of her left knee. Meanwhile, I continued to fight the overwhelming feelings of nervousness that our dope was going to spill into the floorboard.

"Stop moving, Chloe."

"I'm trying. Honest. But I'm crashing, Bug. Bad."

I grabbed hold of her leg and firmly held it in place. "Well try harder. The sooner you hold still, the faster it'll be ready."

"Okay. Okay."

I let go of her leg, added more water, and continued mixing. Stirring *dirt* into water with a needle was no easy feat. It required diligence and a shit load of patience.

"I've told you already. I can't go score more dope right now."

"Well, I can't either," Chloe shot back.

I continued to mix the water and powder together.

I had grown suspicious of her quick excuse not to pitch in for *dirt* should we need to score more.

"Why can't you earn? You've only had two Johns today."

Chloe opened and closed her mouth several times. "I think I got lockjaw from the last guy."

"He a regular?"

"Maybe."

"What name does he go by?"

"I call him Mr. Took Too Damn Long."

I carefully removed the spoon off Chloe's knee and held it up into the air before sliding the lime green lighter underneath it. I turned towards her and winked. "Yeah, I think I know that guy."

Chloe let out a snorted laugh.

"We call him 'Forever Freddy'. Tall. Slim. Black hair. Beady eyes. Drives a white classic *Cadillac*. Right?"

She nodded her head up and down fast. "Yup. Yup. That's the one."

I smirked. "Forever Freddy. Pays good. But he makes sure you earn every dime."

She rubbed her jaw again. "Yeah, no kidding."

Chloe stared at the spoon like a yearning child at Christmas time over a present.

If only I truly understood that feeling. I was lucky if I got a 'Merry Christmas' from momma. Never mind a present. I used to see and envy the happy kids I saw with their families I watched at the mall as they took pictures on Santa's lap and got to tell him what they wanted for Christmas.

In our trailer, it was Christmas year-round. Momma's perverted boyfriends always pulled me onto their laps. The only difference: they told me what they wanted, not the other way around.

"Blech."

"What's wrong, Bug?" Chloe asked.

I had accidentally reacted to my bad memories in her presence.

"Just a bad burger or something."

"Oh, okay." Chloe resumed her mediation breathing routine she always did before shooting up.

I recalled how each Christmas eve, I left Santa Claus a list of what I wanted. My requests were never demanding. I always asked him for love, time with momma, for momma to quit drinking, and to stop bringing nasty men around me.

We rarely had fresh milk in our trailer, so I left Santa, a glass of water and that old can of peas. The same can of peas that had been there since we moved in. I figured maybe Santa could share it with his reindeer. But Santa never brought me shit. Maybe if I had left milk and cookies…maybe.

"Whatever."

"What did you say, Bug?"

"Nothing, petal head. Keep exhaling your bad ju-ju out."

"Oh, okay."

I resumed cooking the mix.

One year I drew a little Christmas tree on my bedroom wall with a broken crayon. I put my newspaper dolls next to it. The only gifts I recycled and gave to myself year after year until I outgrew them and Santa Claus. Santa had been a constant no-show. Wonder if he knew my daddy? He was a no-show in my life, too.

Chloe and I sat in those worn-out car seats for what felt like an eternity. Our eyes heavily fixated on the spoon and flame as they worked together in harmony for our pain-relieving benefit.

Chole rubbed both of her cheeks, "Oh, my jaw hurts. I think I got lockjaw."

"You know you can't get lockjaw from doing that thing with 'Forever Freddy'. I've told you a hundred times, if they can't deliver in five minutes, you're done. Forever Freddy could put you out of business for hours while you heal up. That's a lot of lost earnings. Why do you think we all try and avoid him every time his car is spotted? Huh?"

"But…"

"Listen, kid. I've also told you a hundred times, lockjaw comes from Clostridium tetani. Not doing that." I pointed at her jaw. "But you can get other things from doing that, just so you know."

Chloe recoiled. "Ack! Gross, Bug! I don't like to think about it."

"Well, you need to think about it because it's true. Lots of ooey, gooey yucky stuff. Germs. Bacteria. Fungus. People are flat nasty with washing themselves. Putting their privates in all sorts of dirty places."

Chloe attempted to cover her ears. "I'm gonna puke. Stop it, Bug."

"I'm just sayin'."

I was astounded by Chloe's naivete after being on the streets for a bit. One could lightly toss a stone out the window of a passing car on Nebraska Avenue and hit plenty of working girls who got side-lined due to an STD.

Some girls ignored medical advice and overall consideration. They were junkies. Or, they had a pushy pimp who forced them work regardless and continue to spread the "love" until they were too rank or sore to earn further.

While other girls on the streets easily viewed catching STDs as a game of 'tit for tat', *"I caught it from a John, so I'm gonna give it back to a John. Fucking pigs!"*

Chloe stared at me wide-eyed like I was an all-knowing Guru. "You're so wise, Bug."

"About what?"

"Lots of things."

"Yeah. Sure. Okay." I refocused my attention back onto the spoon and flame. Chloe decided to add a small braid on the left side of her face.

I do not understand how or why Chloe found me wise. I was far from it. I did not know much at all. Sure, I picked up a few things along the way; some basic knowledge, an STD or two and a good street dumpster recipe. But my life tended to resemble that of a bird. I winged it.

I watched Chloe as she gently swayed her head side to side up against the seat rest. Lost in a maze of fantasy.

I thought, *'Too much exhale and not enough inhale… of oxygen."* She tenderly said, "I wish I could be you sometimes, Bug."

I abruptly replied, "No, you don't, kid. Trust me."

Before Chloe could respond, I looked down at the spoon and knew the *dirt* had been cooked enough to bake us both into a short-term oblivion.

"It's done."

Chloe let out a huge sigh of relief. *"Ohhhhh."*

I drew up the freshly prepared liquid into separate needles

I handed a needle to Chloe, "One for you."

She nodded her head like a grateful hippie and said, "Peace and love, my street sister."

"One for me." I gave the needle a flick of the fingers to release any trapped air bubbles.

I had begun preparations to shoot myself up when Chloe stopped me. "Wait. You can't do it yet, Bug."

I was momentarily confused and hoped she was not going to whine again about any uncertainty of the drug. "Why?" I asked.

"You forgot to do me first. Remember?"

"Yes, I remember. I didn't forget." I had actually forgotten. I was in such a rush to get numbed. I forgot about Chloe's phobia.

"You know I hate needles." Chloe then gave me her best irresistible 'pretty please' pout.

Yet another Chloe mystery for the books. How could a junkie who shot up drugs not be able to stick the needle into their own damn vein?

Chloe was my street sister. I had her back. She desperately needed to be set free from her emotional pain. Pain, she thought she kept well hidden by cloaking it with consistent happiness with her hippie jive routine. But I knew better.

Chloe assured me she had dealt with her past. But I knew Chloe was a liar. She was just like the rest of us junkies. I understood why she lied. Abuse hurts. Remembering it. Talking about it. What better way to hide a revolting past than to enter the current world of denial. A place where happiness thrives and lies are just lies you convince yourself are the truth about your newfound street life.

Pain such as Chloe's never fled with the snap of the fingers. Nor could it be ignored, no matter how hard one tried to pretend it did not exist. Life altering pain will remain silent until a weak moment. It is then the pain pounces upon the person's brain, soul and heart until they fall onto their knees and beg for a guillotine to shut the pain up for all eternity.

Freedom for those who run from pain comes in the form of our favorite type of guillotine. Drugs. Only out of ignorance, whether deliberate or innocent, drugs were just a pathetic mirage. There was no freedom with using drugs to silence pain. Our *'so-called-freedom'* came at a high price.

The cost of getting physically hurt while earning.

The cost of getting drugs that might kill you.

The cost of being killed for your drugs or money.

The total cost of what drugs took on your body, inside and outside.

Freedom?

Hardly.

We were each locked in our own prison. To be paroled meant one had to be brave enough to face their inner demons. Get clean. Leave the streets. Or remain stuck in the confines of this prison of hell until an eventual overdose.

But the fear of an overdose was forever trumped by *dirt's'* ability to squash the pains of the past. The basic mindset was,

'Well, it might happen to you. But it will never happen to me. I can handle it. So, it's worth the risk to march towards the guillotine and silence the pain if only for a little while. Off with her head!'

"I forgot. Sorry."

Chloe smiled and handed her needle over.

"Look away, Petal head. I got you."

I tied a shoestring around her left arm and then shot Chloe up. She immediately fell under the enticing embrace of *dirt* and melted into the passenger car seat.

"Definitely out of sight stuff, Bug."

I untied the black shoestring from Chloe's arm and tried to fix myself next. The veins in both of my arms were not cooperating. Typical hassle for a true junkie. Blown veins. I was forced to be creative.

"Between the toes it goes."

And so that sweet, brown-sugar delight went inside my veins, smooth as butter. At first, anyway. It was not long before the unbearable temporary pain of the location I had chosen for the injection set in.

"Ouuuuuuuuuuuch!"

My left foot recovered, as I too melted into the car seat beside Chloe.

At first, the trek was serene.

But soon, the monsters from my past crawled out from the walls.

Snarled teeth.

Bad breath.

Groping hands were felt running all over my body.

"Momma's men," I mumbled. *"Get away from me. Don't touch me!"* My hands pushed at their ghostly hands.

I was in the throes of a bad ride.

Shit!

No one could help me escape the road I walked upon. I had to save myself. Only question…did I want to be saved?

My mind played horrific, taunt-fueled tricks, as the *dirt* surged throughout my body.

First, I saw men.

Lots of men.

From my past.

From the present.

From the past again.

Back to my present.

Then, my past on the streets.

Men were everywhere.

I was surrounded.

Submerged by them.

I felt their hands.

I felt their hot, smelly liquor-scented breath on my neck.

I shuddered.

Suddenly I saw an insect who dug like a maniac in earthly brown dirt. Its small legs worked overtime as it dug and dug. The hole grew deeper and deeper. The pile of dirt it kicked up mounted higher and higher. The bug bore deeper and deeper into the ground.

I begged, *'Let me join you. Please!'*

My mind jumped back and forth between both scenarios.

The men.

The insect.

The men.

The insect.

Over and over.

My soul thrashed about in torment. Pure hell.

My mind thought, *'Dirt, what is wrong with you? You are always my fortress. You deaden my damaged soul. You purge those painful memories from my past. You erase the sensations of filthy hands groping at my ripe, tender breasts. You dull the feeling of rough fingers prying apart my delicate flower, petal by petal. You blur the sight of countless smug, selfish faces who have climbed on top of me. You have hushed my inner screams upon penetration. You deafened my ears to the echoes of fast panting climatic breaths. And you numbed my nostrils of the putrefying scent of hormonally charged pheromones. All my life I have loathed men. And, yet all my life men have lusted after me. A mere glance from a man prevailed my desire to dig deeper into the comfort you always offered. But not on this journey. What changed between you and I, dirt? Why the betrayal?'*

My mind snapped back and concentrated upon the insect who dug. I watched as the insect bore deeper into the ground until it got swallowed up by the actual dirt of the earth and took the many men from my past and present along with it..

An epiphany arose from within.

The collapse had not occurred due to the depth of the hole dug by the insect. But rather the instability of the hole itself. I saw this vision as a foreshadowing of the inevitable downfall of my own life. The bug in the scenario was me. The stark revelation of my grim future caused my high to wind down.

I had dug myself into a dark hole where I was buried alive. Despite suffocating under the weight of each spec of soil, I still managed to breathe. How?

The Prodigal Daughter Flees

I felt as if I died on the inside with each injection. *Dirt* was never going to release me from its firm grasp. Not without a one hell of a fight.

I knew it.

I despised it.

But it was the bold truth.

I was to blame for the mess my life had become. So, I thought. Momma's men never forced me take drugs. The only needle they stuck into parts of my body were the needle in their pants. No syringe dared to touch my veins until I decided when.

The disgusting, unspeakable things their pants needle did to me as a child, sent me down a treacherous road that was hard on my soles and my soul.

When *dirt* introduced itself, suddenly the rough pathway I walked all those years suddenly felt smoother. It lent a softer touch and caressed the bottoms of my feet. It offered comfort to my spirit. I foolishly embraced its false security and assurance. I believed if I remained on the trail with it, *dirt* and I united, no more troubles would befall my life's journey. And if it should, *dirt* would whisk the strife away from my soul.

Dirt could be an entitled bastard when forced to let someone go. I feared ending up like LaRue. A girl who succumbed to *dirt's* sadistic trickery in a seedy alley. I also feared becoming strangled to actual death because of *dirt's* firm grasp on me. I did not want to be found alone in a random back alley, dumped in a ditch by a scared John. Or worse, unrecognizable because no one noticed I had been missing for weeks.

I failed to reason out my fears and courage to continue my dance with *dirt* simultaneously. I dealt with abandonment issues for a long time. I suppose *dirt* feared abandonment, too. Maybe that was how I managed to succeed.

I acted tough as nails on the outside. But inside I was full of painful rusted holes. I prayed for death to put me out of my misery before I was ever forced to breakup with *dirt*. Death for a junkie over a breakup was always the easy way out. No responsibility. No accountability. No withdrawal suffering.

But I was deeply enslaved to *dirt*. It had me tight by the tail. The same as it once had LaRue. Its grip was strong, tight and unrelenting. I tried to breathe but could never quite inhale enough oxygen. I felt braindead.

Every day progressed into a tug-of-war. Part of me desperately wanted to dump *dirt* and never look back. Yet, another part of me could not resist *dirt's* persuasive charms whenever internal trouble brewed and bubbled over. I instantly fell prey to it every single time.

How could I resist?

How could I be so weak?

Pathetic?

Helpless?

Needy?

Easy.

Dirt always helped me to forget.

Everything.

Anything.

Sometimes nothing.

To me, and others like me, *dirt* was a great catch.

A good boyfriend.

Lover.

BFF.

Parent.

Boss.

Doctor.

Shrink.

Anything you wanted or needed *dirt* to be.

It just was.

It always would be.

My aqua blue painted eyelids fluttered as they struggled to open and remain as such. I needed to get my bearings. I had absolutely no clue where I was. How I got there. Or, how long I had been there. Unfortunately, I still knew who I was.

'A worthless piece of shit! Whore! Junkie! Loser! Nobody!'

The persistent closure of my eyelids took the lead as I struggled in vain to keep them open. In between hard blinks, my eyeballs glimpsed the sun. Its rays glared through rustled leaves from the big oak tree which towered over me. The tree looked down at me like a disappointed parent.

'Stop staring at me, jerk! It's rude!' I mumbled to the tree.

The sun rays stung my eyeballs again. Its beams felt like drops of acid with each forced peek-a-boo glance I took.

Light.

Dark.

Light.

Dark.

Light.

Dark.

I shifted my glance to the right and saw a marque sign which read, *Holy Redeemer Church* in big, bold black letters. I was somewhere near Hanna Avenue. My drugged-up ass apparently passed out in the flowerbed of a church.

'Well Hallelujah, Bug!'

I lay flat on my back, on top of a bed of gorgeous yellow Coreopsis and pink Petunias. I resembled a disheveled weed.

Messy haired. Smeared make-up. Stinky armpits. I absolutely reeked of cigarettes and stale greasy fries. Yet, another night of tricking, binging and *'I can't remember what the hell else I did or didn't do'* tucked underneath my *'I'll regretfully remember it one day belt'*.

"Bet you're proud of me now, huh, God?" I whispered, before I gave a thumbs up towards the sky.

The tree appeared to stare down at me again. Only this time, the look it offered was one of pity.

"Stop staring at me you pile of dehydrated toothpicks," I snapped out, before I turned my back on the tree and curled up into the fetal position. I needed more sleep.

I noticed the white building before with its giant cross mounted on the roof which glowed at night. The church caught my eye many times as I strutted up and down Nebraska Avenue during a John-fueled, drug-seeking prowl. I often tried to shield my eye away from the building due to the overwhelming shame it brought to my doorstep. I felt awful about myself and everything I had done.

"Like looking in a shattered mirror," I mumbled.

For years I purposefully avoided going anywhere near the church, or any church. Many times, I received invitations from non-judgmental church folk to come and join. But I declined. I feared churches. It was the whole brimstone and fire thing.

Plus, the years I had been told what an abomination and mistake I had been since birth. Momma made certain to sear that thought deep into my brain before she died. My relationship, or non-existent relationship with churches and God was void.

'Dirt, you clever bastard. You are the one who brought me to this church didn't you. Why? Are you trying to dump me? Do you not want to be there for me anymore? Have you stopped loving me?'

I assumed God was persistently disappointed and pissed at me. I swore there were times I felt His anger and other times I felt His love. If only for a fleeting second. But it was not enough to convince me that love was stronger than disappointment and anger.

One casual glance at my whorish, junkie, raped, molested, momma wished I had never been born, lifestyle was all the proof I needed to justify any wrath he chose to thrust upon me. I deserved it, too. I was the one to blame for a pathway to hell, after all.

My countless mistakes in life had begun with being breast fed as a baby instead of by bottle. Momma's milk was a White Russian served at the local titty tavern. She once said, "You only kept my pickled milk down. You puked up formula." Further proof I was destined for a shit-stained life.

"Where were you God when I really needed you?"

No sooner had those words tripped over my chapped, dried lips, when the dark brown door to the *Holy Redeemer Church* opened. A young priest stepped out onto the smooth white concrete steps. I froze like a snowman about to be melted by a blow dryer if I dared move.

I remained in the fetal position and squinted my eyelids tight. No light filtered in. Natural or Godly. I felt disgusted with myself. Unworthy to be in the presence of a priest. The presence of God. The presence of the church building. The feelings of condemnation were strong. I even felt unworthy to be in the presence of the flowers and the giant judgmental tree. I felt utterly worthless and flat gross.

I heard the priest's soft, gentle footsteps. They grew louder as he slowly approached. I was nervous on the inside but remained silent and very still on the outside. I slowed my breathing to a super shallow mode. I appeared dead.

The priest bent down.

I tensed up.

I feared what he might do.

The possibilities were endless given my life experiences.

Most men were not noble.

Clothed or otherwise.

I peeked ever so subtly out of my left eye.

I watched as the young priest looked me over.

I wanted to shudder at his glance but hesitated.

What did he want with me?

Mercy?

A mercy screw?

Did he pity me?

I peeked at him again.

His eyes dropped towards my chest.

I thought, *'I knew it! A pervert! Stop staring at my chest!'*

But then something changed.

He stared back up at my face and leaned closer.

I tensed up even more.

The priest was searching for signs of life.

He was not a pervert.

So I hoped.

The priest appeared genuinely concerned and uncertain if the girl lying in his church's flowerbed were dead or alive. I relaxed, when the priest suddenly reached forth, placed his hand upon my shoulder, and rolled me onto my back. He then shook me.

"Hello," he said, then shook me again.

At first, I was unsure of how to react. *'Do I come around? Do I punch him in the face and run away? Do I spit at him? What should I do?'*

My immediate instinct was to clock him hard in the face and go on a cussing rant about keeping his filthy hands off my body. But he was a priest. But he was also still a man underneath that pristine uniform. I found myself in an awkward situation.

I had never encountered a real priest before. At least not knowingly. But Johns do lie about themselves. For all I know, I could have slept with one or two. Who knows. Only God, I suppose.

He shook me again.

I remained still.

I honestly did not know how to respond to this man.

"Hello. Hello," he repeated and gave my shoulder another firm shake. "Hello. Can you hear me? Are you alright?"

I had grown nauseous from so much movement. I needed to do something before I puked or got arrested.

"Hey. Are you alright?" He asked me again, only a bit louder.

'It's now or never. Get your fists ready, Bug, just in case.'

I slowly *fake* opened my eyes. Closed them. Then opened them again. My head felt like a thousand ants tap danced all over it. It felt itchy and painful at the same time. My brain felt like it had been dipped in formaldehyde. My stomach wanted to empty. My bladder did, too.

I wondered, *'What's the priest going to do with me?'*

In my best *'out of it sounding voice'* I replied, "Huh? What?" I then half-rubbed my eyes and tried to focus before I sat up.

In a concerned tone the priest asked once more, "Are you alright?"

I said nothing. I just stared at him and then upwards at the tree that scowled back down at me for playing games with the kind priest.

I tried to sit up but fell back down. My body was not as awake as I had originally thought.

"Here, let me help."

Even though I did not want to be touched, I welcomed the priest's hand onto my left wrist as he helped pull me upwards.

"What happ...," I started to ask, when the priest reached forth and touched the same shoulder as before.

'Big mistake!'

This time, I reacted tartly and smacked his hand away.

"Get your Godda…" I stopped myself from finishing the crude reply.

He instantly retreated. "Sorry. I'm sorry."

"It's cool. Just don't touch me anymore. Okay? Unless you want to pay for something. Then…" I eyed him up and down with a coy smile.

The man was young, slightly older than I, but still young. But he was a priest. A dedicated man of the cloth. A man married to God. But a man is a man, nonetheless. I felt oddly compelled to be a bitch in his presence. To me, this priest's kindness was probably a mirage left over from last night's drug bender.

I allowed my loose shirt to purposefully slide off my shoulder and raised both eyebrows in a flirtatious manner. "Well? Do you wanna touch…"

"I…ummm…I…," he stammered. The priest blushed and cleared his throat. Clearly uncomfortable.

'Mission accomplished. Not a pervert.'

"It's okay." I pulled my shirt back up and jokingly added, "I didn't think so anyway. But it was worth a shot. I gotta go."

I gathered up my things. My filthy blue dumpster purse. A half-smoked pack of cigarettes. An extra concert shirt of some shitty boyband I kept on hand in case I puked or got puked on and needed to change in a pinch. And my infamous lime green lighter.

I lost my balance on the way to standing up and instinctively leaned half-way into a strong hedge until my composure was regained. I dropped the lime lighter during the fumble. I went to retrieve it, when the priest beat me to it. He picked it up and handed it back to me.

"Thanks." I then lit up a cigarette and took a deep drag. It was then I noticed the priest had kind eyes.

"You're welcome," he replied.

As I remained fixated on his ocean blue eyes, I almost felt like a normal person. A person who never whored, used drugs, was pure and ever messed with. A person with goals. Hopes. Dreams. But my dreams had long ago morphed into well documented nightmares

I thought, *'I wonder what his name might be. David? Mark? Perhaps, Luke? It's probably just Father. They're all called 'Father'. Lucky me. I have daddy issues. A perfect divine appointment if ever. Screw you dirt for bringing me here.'*

I took another deep drag and rustled the back part of my greasy, dirty-blonde hair with my left hand. It was then I embarrassingly noticed the fresh, visible track marks on my arm.

'Crap! The priest probably saw them, too.'

I pretended to scratch an itch on my back to hide my tracked-up arm. It was not a full-on lie. I did have an itch. *Dirt.* And the desire to scratch it needed to be satisfied. Soon.

I felt ashamed. Weak. Pathetic. No right to exist. Too unpure to have set foot upon church property. Who did I think I was? I had no right to be in the presence of a man who loved God. A man who knew God so intimately. A man who believed in His existence. The priest was a pure man. He was a clean man.

I felt like a wash rag taken from its clean packaging and used up until I was covered in dirty, putrefied liquids and various rotten particles picked up along the way. My fabric now worn so thin I was ready to disintegrate at any moment.

I took another drag off my cigarette. "Can I ask you a question?"

"Of course." His voice sounded compassionate. Unlike the gruff, graveled voices of the chain-smoking, hard-drinking Johns I was accustomed to hearing.

Their disgusting requests.

Their loud grunts.

Their fast-paced moans.

Their endless grumbles when it came time to pay.

My guilt-ridden eyes averted away. I struggled to gain the courage to ask my question. I blamed momma. She always made me feel stupid every time I opened my mouth and spoke. Her boyfriends on the other hand made me shy. But not in a cute, good way. More like the, *if I speak, I will get hurt and messed with even more ways*.

"It's just that…well…well…" I stammered.

"It is alright. Take your time, child."

'Child? Child? Child? Oh, God. He sees me as a child.'

Fire ignited in my eyes over being called a child. My soul seethed. I never wanted to be a child again. Ever! I would rather burn in hell.

I half-yelled, "I ain't no one's child."

"I'm sorry. It's just a term. I did not mean to upset you."

I glared at him.

"What shall I call you?"

"Nothing," I bitterly snapped back. "Child. Child. CHILD!" I started to work myself up again. The priest appeared frightened and unsure of what to do. "Are you fu…nevermind."

"I'm sorry. I won't say it again. Please forgive me."

I took a drag from my cigarette and calmed down. "Whatever."

"What is it you wish to know…" He began.

"Bug."

He nodded his head once. "Bug. What is it you wish to know, Bug?"

I paused. He said nothing. He dawned the patience of a saint. After a few more moments of *'Chloe type silent treatment'*, I replied, "What did I do wrong?"

"Wrong? What do you mean, what did you do wrong? Do you mean sleeping in the flowerbed?" He gestured his right arm towards the semi-smushed bed of flowers. "You did nothing wrong. It happens more than you think. This place…"

"What about this place is so damn special."

"Not special. Peaceful. Anyone is welcome."

"Anyone?" I asked with skepticism.

"Anyone. We're all God's children."

I grew angry again. "I'm not anyone's child." I readjusted my purse strap on my left shoulder. "Never mind. Forget it. I need to go."

I felt the urge to flee. I sensed the priest about to open my pandora's box. Though I knew what contents the box held, what I did not know was what my reaction might be to their reveal. Or, if I would be able to repack any of it back into the box.

"Wait. Please. Don't go," he begged.

I felt dumb in that moment. I sensed momma laughing her dead ass off at me for talking to a priest. I changed my mind. I no longer wanted to know the truth about what I had done wrong. If time had taught me one thing, it was ignorance is bliss.

Why did I need an answer in the first place. I had done wrong all my life. Momma said as much. Plus, I did drugs. I abused my body. I slept with countless men. Momma did not love me. My father walked out on me. I endured endless sexual abuse. The list of condemnations rolled onward and downward. Like a filthy snowball growing bigger by the minute.

I turned away to bolt. The priest grabbed ahold of my left hand. When I looked back, I was shocked. There stood a man who was not angry that I wanted to leave his presence. He was not upset that I had yelled at him. What remained was a man with kind eyes. I was unsure of what to do. I never met a man who only wanted to help me, not help himself to me. It was new.

"Please," he said.

I hesitated. "I really gotta….you know…I gotta…" I pointed in the opposite direction.

"Go?"

I gave a sheepish gaze. "Something like that. Yeah."

"I understand. But can you sit for just a moment.?" He pointed at the concrete stairs in front of the church entrance. "Please. I would like to try and answer your question."

I released a huge, very loud *sigh* bathed in annoyance, before I reluctantly followed this kind man over to the stairs. I sat beside him, as he continued to hold onto my hand.

I remained on the stairs, locked inside my own private room of silence.

"Do you trust me?"

I scoffed and jerked my hand out of his. "Trust you? I don't even know you. You're probably just some prick," I corrected myself. "Sorry…some guy who…well I don't know what you want from me."

"Not everyone is bad."

"Not everyone is good."

He tried to take hold of my hand again but failed.

I grew spiteful, "You think you can help me, huh?"

"I would like to at least try."

"Okay, *'Mr. I want to help the wounded druggie whore'*, answer me this; Why do men like to make the letter J for me since I was a little girl?"

His reaction was one of perplexion. "The letter J?"

I lit up a fresh cigarette. "That's what I said. The letter J."

"I'm afraid I don't understand."

I immediately stood up. "I knew it. Men. You're all liars. Phonies. Help me, my ass. You damn well what I'm talking about."

"Can you please tell me what you mean by the letter J. I'm afraid I'm a bit confused," he nervously replied. For whatever reason, maybe because he was a priest, I believed his confusion. He appeared sincere. I sat back down on the stairs beside him.

"Why have men always liked me in that, you know, way all my life?"

I pulled my hair behind my ears and hugged my knees up to my chest. I turned to my left and noticed the priest looked sad.

'Why did this man care what other men did or had done to me since I was little? Did he really love all of mankind same as God?'

The priest took both of my hands in his and proceeded to answer my question the best way he could. Unfortunately, my rebellious, angry attitude, along with anxiety of learning the truth that it might have been my fault all along, caused me to block out his answer consciously. Though my subconscious had other plans and secretly retained his words.

The priest rambled on for what seemed like an eternity.

My bladder was about to burst. My stomach was starving. And I still had a *dirt* itch which needed scratching.

I thought, *'Hurry up so I can go already.'*

I finally caught a break when a car horn honked, and I snapped out of whatever Led Zeppelin song I forced to play inside my head the entire time the priest spoke. It was then I heard him say, "God loves you so much, child."

The moment I heard the word child again, tears started to well up in the corners of my eyes. The bad memories of my childhood flooded forth. I panicked and jerked my hands from the priest's.

"Don't call me child! I hate that fucking word!"

I then ran away as fast and as hard as I could. I ran from the young priest, the church, God. All of it.

Pull Me Under

Light.

Dark.

Light.

Dark.

Light.

Dark.

The sun's rays burst forth across the surface of the rolling Hillsborough River. Its reflection nearly blinded anyone who glanced its way. The sun acted as a shepherd. The beams, its staff, protected its flock from grazing too close to the river's edge.

Many dangers lurked beneath the murky surface of that riley waterway. Alligators. Undercurrents. Big fish. Small fish. Crabs. Various items of trash. Snakes. Vegetation. Contaminants. And the occasional Bull Shark. Whether on land or in a boat, I realized nowhere was truly safe in the Tampa Bay area.

It had been a week or so since I encountered the young priest. He was the only man I ever crossed who wanted nothing from me. He wanted to give, not take and help guide me towards a path towards redemption.

'Whatever that meant.'

Since our fateful meeting, I tried my best to sack his words deep inside my mental *file thirteen* to be silenced forever. While I appreciated his kindness, I had little to no faith for any possibility of changing my life.

I felt the young priest had wasted his precious breath on me. My life was destined to end sooner rather than later. I saw no point in changing my trajectory. I was a whore. That was not going to change. I was also a junkie. Not going to change that, either.

It's not that a part of me did not long for change. I was just not ready to let go of *dirt*. *Dirt* was not ready to release me either. I found a sick, twisted comfort in that revelation. Or deception, as I am certain the young priest would have emphasized regarding my lost soul.

I had traveled alone around the Tampa Bay area since a spontaneous decision I made the last time Chloe and I got high together. The same day I met the young priest.

I woke up the following morning and simply wandered off. I never spoke to Chloe about it. As I stared out over the river, I recalled how angelic and sweet she looked the last time I saw her. Like a sleeping bunny, as I, the seedy serpent, slithered away coated in the diamond patterned skin of a coward.

I felt restless, discontented and agitated. Over a week was the longest I had been away from my street sister, ever. The only other time I abandoned Chloe was when she was arrested for panhandling. I could not afford bail. And because *dirt* came first, Chloe remained in jail over a long holiday weekend until her court hearing.

Chloe was lucky. The judge, being a prior hippie himself, took an immediate shine to her. Who did not love Chloe? Sure, she could grind on your nerves with all that *peace and love* jive. But at the end of the day, her heart was pure gold. The judge saw it, too. Her feathered headband. Her love for *Led Zeppelin*. Her love for one another outlook. He dismissed her case on the spot.

Later, we celebrated at the Beans & Jellies Café. Pop hooked us up with the best chocolate covered chocolate donuts in town. And all of the coffee we could drink.

I worried about Chloe. I hated being away from her. I was concerned about her innocently wandering the harsh streets of Tampa Bay alone. I was not by her side to protect her from shady Johns. Chloe's kindness and naivete had gotten her in serious, dangerous trouble more than once. I hated not being there to protect her, as always. I hoped she was safe. I was a selfish jerk for taking off without a word. But I had to be alone. I needed space to sort shit out.

As I meandered around Tampa Bay, I struggled to comprehend what fueled such a disconnected attitude inside of me. A need to rumble aimlessly about the concrete jungle alone. Though I was naturally disconnected from others by choice, this time the desire felt even more intense. Grinding. Unrelenting. It felt like a hundred chickens pecking at a little black blemish on my soul. I had to figure things out. Soon.

'I have to get back to, Chloe.'

I worked despite my mysterious restlessness. Quick tricks, only. I loathed being touched even more now than before. But I had to feed the withdrawals. As the sun rose the next day, my entire body sank. I felt very unwell. *Dirt's* subtle reminder who was truly in control.

'Definitely not you, skank bait!' I thought. I then fumbled through my purse to find the only thing to fix that which ailed me.

I snuck behind a bush and shot that sweet, brown colored, sugary delight, between my toes. The amount was not nearly enough to get bombed into an oblivion. Which I needed. But I could not afford to pay. It was the price one waged when not turning enough tricks. Tiny refused to front anyone.

"Dammit, Bug! Every. Damn. Time," I harshly bitched out loud at myself. "Idiot!"

I bled between my toes. I normally could have cared less. But I borrowed Chloe's boots without asking. I left a pair of raggedy sneakers behind in their place. She was going to be pissed. And even more pissed if I returned her boots in the condition befitting of a crime scene on the inside.

I hobbled my way down to the Hillsborough River's edge to wash my bare feet off in the cool, crisp water. I was concerned an alligator might smell the blood and tear my foot off. However, I feared Chloe's wrath more. So, I took the risk.

The sun felt strong, and its rays glared hard as I approached the shoreline. I hoped I did not step in anything nasty on my way down; used needle, used condom, dog shit, etc.

The blades of soft grass were tall and comforted my sore toes. The city had not tended to any landscaping on this side of town for a while. I believed it to be a deliberate attempt by City Officials to hide the true ugliness of Nebraska Avenue and its surrounding areas.

I reached the edge. "Finally!"

I dropped Chloe's precious vanilla Go-Go boots off to the side. The small lapping waves washed up on shore and sounded soothing. I was struck by the reflection of myself as it bounced on top of the river's surface. I shook my head side-to-side and fought back tears.

"Who the fuck are you anymore, Bug? Do you even know?" I muttered.

I despised the disgusting, unrecognizable reflection that stared back at me. I reached for a small rock close-by and threw it hard at the mirrored image.

I shouted, "Whore!"

The rock was not strong enough to curb the fit of self-hate I experienced. I spit at my reflection, too. By now, blood had pooled beneath my toes. Larger, cold waves caused by the thrown rock washed up and placed gentle kisses on the tips of my filthy toes.

"*Burr!*"

The face of the priest flashed before my eyes as I squatted down to wash off my feet.

I thought, '*No one ever noticed my broken, battered spirit hidden behind my two crystal blue irises.*'

I momentarily paused. '*But he saw me. The real me. The me I so longed to be, but never could.*'

I washed my feet harder.

'*His kind words. His soft stare. My soul was naked before him. The most naked I had ever been. My naked soul felt unashamed. Every spot, blemish and wrinkle of life exposed without judgement. None of my own self-disgust repelled him. It did not turn his gaze away. Nor did it cause his private parts to stir with wicked desire. He was not like the others. For a moment I swore I had seen God's love for me in his eyes.*'

The more I thought about the priest and our conversation about God and His love for me, the harder I tried to scrub the spiritual and physical filth away from my flesh.

I grumbled, "*The letter J.*"

I scrubbed even harder. My violent scrubbing motion caused the silt on the bottom of the river to stir about. I noticed curious fish swim close by. My feelings of revulsion became almost too much to bear. I wondered how those fish tolerated being near such a putrid existence.

I hissed out, "Jezebel is what you are. You, retched whore! It's who you've always been. Momma was right."

A TV preacher who I saw on a TV in a room after a trick with a John popped into my head. I could still hear him as he spoke about a woman in the Bible named Jezebel. A whore who enticed men to sin. This preacher said, "All whores shall burn in hell come judgement day," before he slammed his fist down hard onto a podium. I immediately turned off the TV and hid in the bathroom shower until the John left.

Momma somehow managed to put the fear of God in me, despite not being a true, God-fearing woman herself. Another one of life's great mysteries, I suppose. I did not realize this to be the case until my feet were put towards the fiery furnace. My face shoved into the hellish belly of truth. My soul, prepared to burn to a crisp.

Just the thought of that TV preacher caused me to scrub my skin even harder. I tried in vain to wash the memory away.

"Fuck him! I ain't no Jezebel! They are! All those filthy, rotten, disgusting men!"

I thought, *I never forgot the way the TV preacher described hell. He talked about it before launching into the Jezebel speech. I also recalled the way momma described it, too. The thought of burning in hell scared the crap out of me. But the thought of not being able to squirm on my belly in dirt like the worm I had become was even more frightening. I knew down inside my soul teetered at the brink of brimstone and fire from the sins that were committed all due to the letter 'J'.'*

I shuddered.

The water was cold.

My thoughts, colder.

When I looked down at my foot, it was redder than a vine ripened tomato. My skin felt raw and tender to the touch.

"Oww!" My mind wandered away from the external pain and back to the internal agony.

'The priest said God loved me no matter what bad things I had done. That those inappropriate touches by others weren't my fault. Nor was the path I currently walked upon to try and forget about it all, either. He said I could be someone new. My painful past all but forgotten. I desperately wanted to believe him. I truly did. But I lacked the ability or perhaps the guts to try and find a way to make it so.'

I stood up and looked out at the water.

'But the constant reminder of the vile things I had done. The things I still do. The thing I just did which led me down to the river to wash myself clean…'

I reached down, picked up another rock and threw it out into the river.

'The vile things done to me. I felt gross. Ashamed. I wanted to scream every time I was touched. But my lips would never part. My voice always grew mute. My tongue twisted up. My throat tightened. Fear emerged from a dark place. It grew, and grew, until there was no longer any room left for my lungs to draw a meager breath. So, I turn and run.'

"I'm still running. I probably always will."

I stared down at my distorted, rippled reflection in the river, again and whispered with a tear formed in my eye, *"Maybe."*

Lost

Light…

"Let's move it along. Come on. Scoot, scoot," a police officer said, as he shined his bright flashlight directly into my pea-sized pupils.

I snapped back, "Okay. Okay. Get that fucking thing out of my eyes. I can't see shit."

"Aren't we the cheery one." He then turned his attention at other people who were passed out in the alley and yelled, "Party's over folks. Let's go."

The passageway soon filled with sounds of cussing, coughing and one unlucky person retching.

"What time is it?" I asked.

"Time to get moving."

"No kidding. What actual time is it?" I inquired as I gathered up my things.

He shot a look of disgust in my direction. "For you, I'm sure it's five o'clock somewhere."

I stared at him, bewildered by such a belligerent attitude. Most seasoned police officers knew us by name and/or by collar. He must have been a transfer from another department. "I don't drink."

"It's four o'clock. Happy."

"No. You woke me up."

"Let's *gooooo* people!" He shone the light on several homeless people's faces as he continued clearing the alleyway. He turned back to me, "Come on. Move it, princess. Stop stalling."

"I'm going. I'm going."

He nudged the foot of a passed out old man. "Come on, Sir. Or it's a comfy night at *Chateau Le Jail* for you." The homeless elder, we fondly called Jerry, waved the cop's threat off and drunkenly stumbled out into the night.

"It's moving day folks. Time to pack your shit and get."

All the drugged up, drunken degenerates, including myself, scattered from the once serene alleyway like wasted cockroaches.

"Thank *yoooooou!*" the officer taunted. He added insult to injury with a sarcastic waving of his right hand. "Nite-nite! Sleep tight. Or it's into the slammer for my delight."

"Asshole," I replied.

"Have a good night, princess."

I stuck my tongue out at him despite wanting to give him the middle finger.

It had been around two weeks since I abandoned Chloe in the car. Despite my time away, I failed to resolve whatever bothered me. That upset me even more. Something still brewed within my craw, and I had no clue how to lower the heat. I decided it was time to give up and return to Chloe.

Chloe was going to be so happy to see me and her prized boots again. How she managed to wear them and not get blisters on her feet was yet another 'Chloe Mystery'. Since my time away, I developed a new appreciation for the raggedy sneakers I had left behind.

The following morning, the first place I checked for Chloe was at the Beans & Jellies Café. I knew she panhandled in front of the building most mornings.

No sign of her. Though odd, it was not out of the ordinary. Panhandling sucked in the area sometimes, so she relocated.

I spotted Paula strutting down Nebraska Avenue. I shouted, "Hey, Paula!"

"Hey, Bug!"

"Have you seen, Chloe?"

Paula shot back, "Haven't seen her! Gotta boogie! I'll let her know you're looking for her!"

"Thanks!"

"You got it! Boogie-fever! Boogie-down!"

My next thought, jail.

"I hope that petal head didn't get herself arrested. I only have enough money to score *dirt*."

I asked Pop if I could borrow the café phone and the white pages.

"Sure," he replied.

"Sorry. There's no Chloe Littlefield here," the jail clerk on the other end of the line said.

"Well, shit," I muttered underneath my breath. "Thanks." I then hung up the phone.

Next, I called the local hospitals. I struck out there, too. No patient named Chloe Littlefield had been admitted.

"Thanks, Pops." I handed the white pages back to him.

"Did you find her?"

"Nope."

Sensing my concern, he reached out and patted my hand in a gesture of reassurance, "You will. Don't you worry yourself." He put a plate before me. "Have a jelly donut. It's on the house." He then gave me a wink and a smile.

I half-heartedly whispered, "Thanks Pops."

I was the most difficult one to find, not Chloe. She could always be found. I stared at the yellow telephone and waited for it to ring with an answer.

"Where are you, kid?" I asked of the still phone. No response. I released a sigh, grabbed the donut and exited the café.

I needed to meet Tiny and score, so I took a break from hunting down Chloe. Between the stress of her absence, to the last time I got high, my withdrawals were on the rise.

Tiny handed me a small plastic baggie with his signature design on it. I took it and shoved it into my back pocket.

I looked side to side, then back at Tiny. "Hey, have you seen, Chloe, Tiny?"

"You mean, Flowerchild?"

"Yeah. Her." My heart picked up the pace. I hoped for a "yes" to my desperate question.

"Haven't seen her in like a week or something, cockroach."

I thought, *'Dammit, Chloe! An entire week? How are you getting by without being sick. I hope you're not lying somewhere by yourself too ill to get help. I must find you quickly.'*

I dug some cash out of my front jean shorts pocket and paid Tiny. I did not have time for further conversation. I had to split.

"If you see her, will you let her know I'm looking for her?"

"You got it."

"Catch ya later, Tiny."

"Scram, cockroach!"

"It's, Bug!" I shouted back.

"Yeah, I know. I know."

Another girl soon walked up to Tiny to score.

I heard him ask, "Whatchu need, baby?"

The only place I failed to search for Chloe at was the abandoned car we fixed up. My stomach flipped at the idea of seeing my smiling hippie street sister at the car anxiously waiting for me. She would have a flowery weed in her hand and Led

Zeppelin IV blasting from the worn-out headphones of her Walkman that hung around her neck.

I rounded the corner and made my way towards the car. I left Chloe there two weeks ago.

"Maybe she never left after I did," I said to myself.

The thought vanished as I immediately noticed no signs of movement in the passenger seat underneath a lump of clothes. I looked up and saw seven buzzards circling in the blue sky above. My legs felt weak, but I forced them to move forward.

"A poncho," I said, as I picked up one of the garments and inspected it. I rifled through the rest of the pile. "Shirts. Dresses. Shorts. Where did you get all this crap, kid?"

I looked around the front half of the car. All appeared intact. Nothing inside appeared to be missing. I carefully peeked into the back seat of the car in case she was in a ball sleeping. No Chloe. Just two messed up bohemian blankets.

I shook my head side to side, "What is going on?"

I plopped into the driver's seat, flipped the visor down, then up and glanced around the inside of the car again. I stared at the *polaroid* picture of Chloe and I, taken in front of the café, placed next to the speedometer.

"Come on kid. Give me something, here."

My eyes aimlessly searched around the inside of the automobile for a clue as to where Chloe might be. Nothing stood out. Then, I remembered Chloe kept a diary. I reached over to the passenger's side of the car and stuck my hand underneath the seat.

"I better not get bit by a spider, petal head. You know how I hate those eight-legged bastards!"

My hand fumbled about and touched various hippie trinkets Chloe kept hidden underneath the seat. Bird feathers, bottle caps, rings and other assorted stuff either found or stolen. Basically, an entire collection of junk she viewed as treasure.

"I know you're here. She never takes you out of the car. Where are you?"

My hand eventually felt something familiar shoved almost into the backseat. "Ah-ha! Gotacha!" I slowly removed Chloe's diary from under the seat. The loose trinkets on top of it, spilled across the floorboard.

"Oops!"

Chloe's diary was a black and white Mead Notebook she wrote random thoughts in. She was extremely sensitive about its contents. I would never have violated her privacy, but I felt this was an emergency. No one had seen her in days. No one had heard from her in days. She was not arrested. She was not hospitalized.

"Shit! I forgot to check the morgue." I suddenly felt sick at the thought of her being dead.

I snorted a dab of *dirt*. Though not my usual method of getting high, it was not my first time doing it that way. I needed a boost of courage to read what Chloe wrote. I did not care what most thought of me. But I did care what she thought. Only I never let her know I did.

"Here we go, kid."

My mind instantly tripped into another dimension as I thumbed my way through the wrinkled, liquid stained pages. There were no dates or times to mark events Chloe journaled. Entries were scattered throughout the book. Her mind was unfocused. The more pages I read, the more various layers of Chloe emerged.

Chloe's Far-Out Feelings

I met a groovy girl today underneath the bridge. Her name's Bug. I don't think that's her real name. But maybe it is. I will ask her. She saved my life today. I could have drowned in the river when I slipped on the ground and almost fell in. No one ever saved my life before. I mean, except for the doctor when I was born. My mom said when I was born, I had low oxygen or something because the cord was wrapped around my neck. I had to stay in the hospital for a while until I felt groovy again. This chick Bug I met is so cool. She's the first person I've met on the streets that hasn't tried to rob me, rape me or beat me up. I'm so happy I met her. I think we're going to be best friends. Maybe she can be the sister I always wanted to have but never got. The end.

My eyes welled up with tears. "Glad I met you that day, too, petal head."

I've been thinking about my mom a lot. I called her last night, and she said I could come home. She misses me. I miss her, too. She said we could work on the house rules together and that she dumped that creep who used to come into my room at night to mess around with me. He thought I was foxy or something. Gross!. I want to go home sooooooo bad. I mean, I love the friends I've made while being on the streets. I would miss them sooooooo much! Especially Bug. Maybe my mom would let me bring Bug home with me. Then we could be sisters forever! She could sleep in the spare room. It's across the hall from my room. Then, when my mom goes to bed, I could sneak into Bug's room where we'd talk and laugh all night and pig-out on ice cream! Gosh, I miss my mom so much. I miss my soft pink bed and my stuffed animals. But I like having no one telling me what to do all the time. Well, except for Bug. But she's my big sister. She's supposed to boss me around. I'm kind of glad she does. I feel loved. Bug is so groovy. The end.

"Why didn't you tell me about being homesick, Chloe? Geez?" I shook my head, dumbfounded by her true feelings sealed in silence. "You miss your stuffed animals, huh? Sometimes I forget you really are still just a kid. What the hell are you doing on the streets? Seriously?"

The more entries I read, the more I realized I did not really know Chloe as well as I thought. Her entire hippie, peace and love routine was a show she put on to everyone. Including me. The reality? She was just a scared, homesick child.

"I feel so stupid. How could I not have seen it?"

Through reading Chloe's diary, I discovered her honest feelings. Shame they had been for the diary's eyes only all this time. I should not have been so surprised. Most people on the streets are never truthful about who they are, how they feel or how they end up on the streets. We all pretend, like professional unpaid actors.

Every.

Single.

One.

Of.

Us.

I read Chloe's second to last entry and hoped for a hint where she might be found.

"Okay. Let's see what you have been up to since I've been gone, petal head."

I don't have enough money to buy stuff from Tiny. He wants too much. Bug's always riding me about going to Tiny only. Tiny! Tiny! Tiny! I'm so sick of being hassled about where I score. My mom always hassled me about how I spent my allowance. Maybe I should leave, Bug and go back home. At least I wouldn't have to hear the name, Tiny anymore. I'm so sick of being treated like a child. She can go off and do whatever she wants, whenever. But if I do it? Noooooooo! That's it! From now on I'm going to do what I want. The end

"Did you go home, Chloe? If you did, why didn't you leave a note or tell someone? Did you leave me out here alone?"

I had become mad at the idea of being abandoned by the only family I had left in this world. I threw the diary across the car. I felt hurt. Discarded.

"Fucking bitch! Who needs you anyway!"

But why was I so angry at Chloe? I had done the exact same thing to her two weeks ago. Left without saying one word. In fact, I had been leaving Chloe for days at a time since we first met.

I took another bump of *dirt* and reached over to pick the diary back up. The faint sounds of emergency sirens wailed in the background. Nighttime had approached. It started to sprinkle rain. I turned the page and landed on what seemed to be a section which contained some of Chloe's final entries.

Woke up today and Bug's gone. She does that sometimes. Disappears on me. I hate it. I feel lonely without her. I'm mad at her. She took my boots without asking. I'll try and make some money today passing out flowers. I saw a yard full of dandelions in front of a house that's been condemned. Hopefully no one has mowed them before I can

185

get there. I haven't been making much money lately and I don't want to trick. But I need drugs, so I might have too. The end.

Bug still isn't back. It's been five days now. How could she leave me for so long? I miss her. I feel so sick. I hope I make enough today begging and handing out flowers at 1275. Things around the café have been dead. Haven't been able to make shit. I need stuff badly. I feel so sick. The end.

Finally, a clue.

My heart leapt for joy. A sense of calm washed over me. Although that particular diary entry was written almost two weeks ago, Chloe decided to remain in that area.

Tomorrow morning, I planned to hitch a ride to the Busch Boulevard exit ramp and look for Chloe. If I had no luck, I would hitch my way over to the Hillsborough Avenue exit ramp, next.

"Hopefully I find you at Busch, petal head."

I resumed reading her diary in search of another clue.

I remember the day Bug and I bought my vanilla boots at the Salvation Army Store. I didn't have enough money, so Bug loaned me some. She knew how much I loved those outta-sight boots. She always knows just what to say or do to keep me high in the clouds. But I wish she hadn't taken them without asking. Her feet are waaaaaaaay bigger than mine. Probably gonna stretch them out wearing them this long. When is she coming back? It's been so long. I need her help.

"So, what are you saying, Chloe? I have clown feet compared to your dainty ballerina toes?" I rolled my eyes. I could just hear her whining about how the boots felt too big now for her tiny feet. I recalled countless times she wanted to go barefoot like a true hippie. But after I explained to her the dangers of stepping on dirty needles, she promised to wear shoes and only go barefoot in our car.

"Deal?"

"Deal."

We then pinky-finger swore on the promise to seal it forever.

Oh, I see Lyla.. Be back soon diary.. The end.

"Who the hell is Lyla?" I asked.

I'm back. Sorry it's been a few days, diary. I was busy with Lyla doing stuff. She's groovy, too. Just like Bug. But she doesn't boss me around and stuff. Maybe because we're the same age.

"What stuff and you and this chick doing, kid? I'm going to have to track this Lyla down and find out what her story is."

Anyway, back to my boot story. Later, Bug and I went to the park and got stoned. It was far out! We did not feel like working. It was such a beautiful day. The sun was shining. I made Bug laugh with my goofy faces. It's not easy to get her to laugh, but I keep telling her how stress is no good for her soul. She needs to ride shit out. Go with the groove.

"What groove took you away from me, huh?"

A group of people were at a nearby pavilion at the park. They were having a party. All I remember is they played some groovy tunes on their radio. I closed my eyes and felt every bit of the rhythm...

I palmed my forehead. "Ugh! Seriously, Chloe? That's such a hippie thing to say, *"Felt every bit of the rhythm."*
The rain started coming down harder.
I heard more emergency sirens wail, only louder.
"Must be a fire somewhere." I resumed reading.

I danced and danced and danced until my feet made me feel like I was floating over the grass. I was flying, like a robin. I did not want to stop, even after the rain started to fall. Bug was mad and wanted to leave. But I grabbed her by the hand and soon we were both dancing and laughing.

The emergency sirens grew louder.

I tried to do a Rockette kick and landed flat on my back. I started laughing as I lay in a puddle of muddy, rainwater. The laughter stopped and Bug

...

I heard a lot of commotion close by. So, I left the diary, leapt out of the car and ran to see what was happening. As I rounded the corner, I saw paramedics running towards a body lying in the middle of a side street in a muddy puddle of rainwater.

"Bug? Bug?" Chloe barely whispered out into the open air, between fading breathes. *"I feel cold, Bug. I'm scared. Why is it getting so..."*

Smack in the Heart

*"…**dark?**"*

My eyes had become fixed on the flashing emergency vehicle lights.

Light.

Dark.

Light.

Dark.

Light.

I watched in horror, along with other spectators, as a lone paramedic performed CPR, while the other paramedic squeezed a blue bag over the person's face. They tried in vain to resuscitate the still person.

The flashing lights drew me in like a moth to an old familiar flame. I unknowingly stepped closer towards the person lying in the street. I was in a trance. My ears detected a gruff sounding police officer's voice, who stood behind me. He forced everyone to step behind the newly placed yellow tape. I ignored his command and continued inching closer to the body.

I was halfway there when a hand grabbed a hold of my arm and yanked me backwards. I turned around and noticed it to be the same cop who had shooed me out of the alleyway the night before.

"Come on, princess. Behind the tape with the other looky-loos. Let's go."

Another police car pulled up. It's headlights glazed across the person in the street. My knees immediately buckled. I violently jerked my arm from the officer's grasp. "Let go of me!" I ran towards the paramedics and shouted, "No! No! No!"

The cop yelled, "Get back here." I continued to run.

"No! No! No! Please, no!" I resumed shouting until I reached…Chloe. It was then I released a wailing scream only a parent releases upon discovering their child on the brink of death or death itself. *"Ahhhhhhhhh!"*

The cop caught up to me and tried to arrest me.

"It's resisting for you, princess."

"Stop! Let me go! That's my sister they're working on."

A paramedic overhead me. "Your sister? Do you know her?"

The cop released one of my arms.

I was out of breath from my fight with the cop and the shock of seeing Chloe lifeless in the street. "I do. I do. Please! Please! Help her!" I then broke completely free from the cop, dropped to my knees beside Chloe. "Don't do this to me, Chloe. Please. You can't leave me. Not like this. Please, Chloe. Not like this."

I tried to hug her, but the cop pulled me back.

"They can't help her if you're in the way."

I sobbed uncontrollably. "Chllllloooooooeeeee! Plleeeasse!"

"What did she take?" a paramedic asked.

I wiped my face and shook my head side to side, "I…I don't know."

I stared down at a motionless Chloe. "What did you do, Chloe? What did you do?" I tried to lunge for her again. And again, I was restrained.

"Stop it or I'm going to put you in the back of my car."

"Fuck you!" I snapped back. "Get your hands off me." I then jerked my arms free from his grasp once more. My uncontrollable sobbing returned.

The paramedics spoke with one another, but I failed to hear what they said. One of the them turned to me and in a stern tone said, "Look. We can't help your friend if we don't know what she took. So, what is it? Smack? Molly? Blues? What?"

I was about to violate Chloe's privacy for a second time today. "Sh..sh…she usually does smack. Sometimes a little weed."

I reached out to hold Chloe's right hand. It was balled up into a fist. The paramedic noticed and pushed my hand away. He carefully undid Chloe's tight fist and discovered a hidden baggie shoved up against her palm. I immediately noticed the logo was not Tiny's. I did not know whose it was or what drugs had been inside of it.

I lunged at Chloe again. I was angry. I got my hands onto her shoulders, shook her and screamed, "What did you take, Chloe? What the fuck did you take? Why? Why? Why didn't you listen to me? Dammit, Chloe! Dammit!"

"That's it," the angered cop snapped out as he snatched me off Chloe and dragged me towards his car. I kicked and screamed violently the entire time.

I looked back and watched the paramedics push Narcan into Chloes arm. She did not respond to it, nor any other attempts of lifesaving.

I thought, *Folks always say you know how you can tell when a junkie is lying? The answer…their lips are moving. It's always the truth…forever wrapped in a convincing lie.'*

We reached the car. I begged the cop to let me return to Chloe.

"Please. She needs me."

"What she needs are paramedics, not another junkie who might give her more drugs."

"Screw you!" I wiggled about. "Get your hands off of me."

He opened the back door, "Get in the car."

"No!"

I turned around and saw the paramedics shock Chloe with the paddles several times but to no avail.

I thought, '*An addict is a lot like the boy in the fairytale, The Boy Who Cried Wolf. Nobody believed the wolf was real because the boy had lied so much about it being real. Much like an addict who says they want to get clean, even though they keep on using drugs in secret. No one believed the boy in the story about the wolf. No one believes in an addict's words, either. No…one…believes…*'

The one paramedic looked towards the police officer and shook his head side to side. I released a guttural cry. "Chloe! Noooooooo!" Chloe was dead.

The cop released me, and I fell to the ground in my own muddy puddle of rainwater. I stared hopelessly and hypnotically at Chloe's body as it rested in the same muddy cold rainwater. She was soon picked up, placed on a gurney and covered with a white sheet. I would never see her smile or hear her kooky words ever again. She was gone. Forever.

I watched a lone feather from her headband fall to the ground and float upon the water in the street. The only evidence of where her soul had departed from the harsh streets of the planet.

The cop decided not to press charges on me. He felt the loss of my street sister was punishment enough. I walked over and retrieved the lone feather Chloe had dropped before the ambulance took her away. I held that feather close to my heart. As I walked past a bar, an all too familiar song blasted from the speakers. Tears rolled down my face as I walked off into the dark, unforgiving night.

"*Fly Robin. Fly. Up, up to the sky.*"

Down

I sat half slumped over, supported by a graffitied concrete Jersey Barrier. An old gray shawl was wrapped around my body for warmth. I was stoned out of my mind on *dirt* and repeatedly blinded by headlights as cars bounced up and down on the rough, pot-holed asphalt towards their intended destination.

Light.

Dark.

Light.

Dark.

Light.

I needed to work, but the last thing I desired was smelly, demanding Johns. I had to numb myself further to get through it. So, I shot more *dirt* between my toes. The veins in my arms and hands were still not healed.

"*Dammit!* That hurts!" I complained, despite the welcomed surge of pain at the injection site. I deserved to be hurt. I failed Chloe.

The sun rose and set fourteen days since Chloe died. I remained in complete denial over it. I never returned to our car after that night. In my mind, if I did not go back, Chloe was alive. Hard as I tried, though my heart knew the truth. It relentlessly ached.

The only true friend, the only real family I ever had on this shithole planet abandoned me. Nothing remained for me to give a crap about anymore… except *dirt*. How I prayed it would not leave me, too.

"Please, don't leave me. I need you. You're all I've got," I rattled off to a baggie coated in the powered remains of *dirt* I had used earlier.

I felt certain Chloe's diary still rested on the passenger seat, exactly where I had left it in the car that fateful rainy night.

I sighed and said, "I watched you arrive to me in the rain. I watched you leave me in the rain. Fuck you rain!"

I momentarily closed my eyes. When I opened them and turned to my right, Chloe was beside me, up against the Jersey Barrier and held onto my left hand.

I stared in disbelief. Half-dazed I asked, "Chloe?" I squinted harder. "Is that really you?"

"It's me, Bug," I heard her reply. The headphones around her neck blared Led Zeppelin's song, 'Stairway to Heaven'.

"But I saw you die that night on the street, in the cold rain."

She shivered. "The rain sure was so cold that night, huh."

"You're here."

"I am."

"How?"

She reached over and touched my heart with her hand but said nothing.

"Where have you been, Chloe? I have missed you so much. I looked for you on Hillsborough Avenue, Busch Boulevard, Fowler Avenue. All up and down Nebraska Avenue. I couldn't …" I stammered, "I couldn't…I couldn't find you. But you're here. You came back to me. You really didn't leave me." My eyes welled up with tears.

"You always worry too much, Bug." She caressed my tear-stained cheek. I stared back at her like a helpless, lost puppy.

"Why, Chloe?"

"Why what?"

"Why did you do it?"

"Do what?" she tipped her head side to side in curiosity.

"Why didn't' you score from Tiny? Was it because of that bitch you met, Lily? Did you trust her more than me, your street sister?"

"Lyla."

197

"Lyla?" I scoffed. "Well, if I ever find Lyla...I swear," I snapped out with gritted teeth.

"Like the song says by *The Youngbloods*, Bug, *we have to love one another right now.*"

I rolled my eyes. "That's such a hippie thing to say, petal head." I then laughed through thick, dripping snot and falling tears. I wiped my nose on the shawl. "I've missed you so much, petal head."

"I know. I'm sorry. You know..."

"Know what?" I asked.

"I've missed you, too."

"I'm sorry I left you that morning. I'm sorry I always went off and left you alone Chloe. I'm such a piece of shit. Why didn't I just stay. You'd still be here and not off with" I changed my tone to sarcastic anger, "Lyyyyy....la. The first part of her name says it all. Lie!"

"It's okay, Bug."

I shook my head side to side and through more snot and tears protested, "No it's not. It's not okay. You're not here anymore, Chloe and it's all my fault." I sobbed uncontrollably. "I miss you so much, Chloe. I don't know how to go on without you. It hurts so much. I hate that you got in."

"Got in where?"

I punched my chest. "Here! In my heart. I worked so hard to keep people out because they hurt me. I trusted you. You hurt me, Chloe. You hurt me when you left. I miss you so much."

"I miss you, too, Bug. Bugging me for this. Bugging me for that. A real pest."

"You're the pest not me, petal head," I teased back. The tears resumed. "Oh, Chloe!"

"*Shh*. Bug. It's okay." She pushed my hair behind my ears. "Here, take this."

I looked downward as Chloe placed an object into my hand. My eyesight was too blurred. "Wha..what is it?"

"Close your eyes, Bug. Listen to the lyrics." The music coming from her headphones had grown louder. "Rest."

I did as Chloe asked. Lyrics from 'Stairway to Heaven' filled the air.

> *And it's whispered that soon if we all call the tune*
> *Then the piper will lead us to reason*
> *And a new day will dawn for those who stand long*
> *And the forests will echo with laughter*

The last thing she spoke before I drifted off into unconsciousness, "I'm with you. I'll forever be with you. I love you, Bug. Peace."

My eyelids opened an hour later and found Chloe no longer by my side. I looked down and noticed a lone feather from her headband rested in the palm of my hand. The same feather I picked up from the street the night she died. The one I barely released from my grasp ever since.

I looked around. "Chloe, come back. Chloe. Chloe! Don't go! I miss you! I need you! Please! Don't leave me!" I begged and panicked through more tears.

Chloe was never there. Her entire visit had been a drug-fueled mirage. The harsh reality of her absence once again became too much to endure.

"Fuck you, heart! It's not true! It's not true. IT'S NOT TRUE!" I shouted.

I cried nonstop and hugged myself as tightly as I possibly could. I shot up again to numb the pain even further. The fresh rush from the *dirt* quickly embraced me. I soon felt less alone as I slid, willingly, into *dirt's* open arms once more for comfort.

I remained slumped up against the cement barrier stoned out of my mind. I continually nodded off, only this time, no vision of Chloe. Instead, I flashed back over the past days of my life since she died.

I passed out at various locations around Nebraska Avenue. Sometimes I woke up with my clothes on. Sometimes naked. Almost every time, absolutely no memory of what happened. I blacked out. I no longer cared what happened to me. I earned enough to buy *dirt* to remain numb and keep Chloe at bay.

I wandered the streets aimlessly in her vanilla Go-Go boots, lost in my own world. The boots were the only tangible thing I had left of her. I felt her presence with every step I took. Each one hurt worse than my cramped-up toes.

"I don't care if you hurt. Keep moving, feet."

I tricked whoever crossed my path for whatever they wanted to pay. Five dollars. Ten dollars. Twenty-five dollars. It did not matter. "Just pay me and fuck off!" were the only words I said to a John, minus, "Yes, I'm available. What do you want? How much you got to pay for it?"

I tried to panhandle, but it never worked out for me unlike Chloe. Maybe because she offered flowers in return for the money. I could never bring myself to pick, nor even look at flowers. It hurt too much.

I rubbed my sore toes where I had shot up. If the area was infected, so what.

I spoke to my foot, "I hope you're diseased. Then you can rot off, along with the rest of my limbs until my soul is finally free and I no longer ache and can be with Chloe again."

I knew I needed to relocate soon. I was certain Officer Dickwad would cruise by the area eventually and threaten to arrest me.

"What do you know about loss? Huh, Officer Dickwad? You don't know shit. That's how much you know. You only know how to arrest people and kick them out of alleyways when they're trying to sleep. No sympathy. No compassion. No idea what the word family means. Like when you kept me from being with Chloe. She was my sister. She died alone, without me holding her hand. And it's all your fault, asshole!" I shouted out at his imaginary image which appeared before my stoned, glazed-over eyeballs. *Dirt* took over and I nodded off again.

Hours later, the sound of a loud horn honk stirred me awake. My eyes were blinded once more with bright headlights.

"Turn your damn brights off, jerk!" I shouted at a green SUV. The driver drove past and never noticed me.

I looked at my left wrist as if I was wearing a watch. "How long have I been out?" I shrugged my shoulders. "Fuck it. Who cares. Time means nothing anymore."

I attempted to stand on my feet but fell. After a few more tries, I held my balance. "Let's *moooooove* it, Princess," I said to myself with sarcasm and then stumbled out onto the street. "Officer Dickwad and the calvary are probably on their way."

Another loud car horn sounded off as I nearly tripped into oncoming traffic. I flipped the bird to the irritated driver in the classic purple dune-buggy and shouted, "Loser!"

I staggered back up onto the sidewalk and glanced around. I was so wasted. I needed to gather my bearings. I was disoriented, but the area felt oddly familiar.

I looked in both directions and asked myself, "Which way should we go, Bug, left or right?" My body lost its balance and leaned towards the right. "Right, it is then. Let's *gooooo*, Princess."

I tripped, stumbled and tumbled about on the uneven sidewalk. The chunky heels of Chloe's boots continued to snag on the bits of broken cement.

A forty-something guy in a blue muscle car approached me. "Hey baby, how much?" he asked.

"Fuck off, loser!" I snapped back.

"Oh, come on baby. Don't' be like that. How much for a good time?"

"Leave me alone, asshole!" I picked up a piece of loose concrete and threw it towards his car. I was so wasted I had no idea if the person was even real or just another figment of my warped imagination.

"Bitch!" He yelled, followed by the sound of screeched tires as he peeled off from the curb.

"Guess you were real. Whatever. I don't give a shit." I laughed and resumed my wasted walk down the sidewalk. "You got the boogie-fever, Princess!"

I was almost past a building, when my eyes were drawn towards a light that flickered from underneath a door. Before I rationalized what I had seen, my feet changed direction, and I found myself headed up a short flight of stairs.

What is happening? I whispered.

Dirty

Light.

Dark.

Light.

Dark.

Light.

The glow from several candle wicks, danced bright orange and yellow flames before my hazed eyes. Their ferocious interpretive dance appeared to say, *"Come in."* I did.

"What is this place?" I asked, as I peered around.

The door clicked loudly behind me. I jumped. "What the…"

I turned around and as my eyes focused, I noticed crosses, stained glass windows, rows of dark wooden pews and a large altar with an oak podium at the front.

"I think this is that church with the kind priest." I shouted, "Hello? Are you here kind priest?"

No one responded.

I shrugged my shoulders, *"Oh, well."*

The air conditioner kicked over. A breeze from the ceiling vent titillated the brightly colored flames of the candles, as they vied for my attention. I looked to my left and saw a side-altar in front of the candles.

In my dazed condition, I spoke to the candles. "Why did you playful little cuties want a whore like me to come in here? Do you want me to get set on fire so I can burn? Do you think I deserve to burn in hell for all the bad things I've done. You know, I belong in the darkness, not the light, right?"

The candles flickered brighter.

"Oh, I think I get it. You think I should be in the light and not the dark, right? Interesting."

I ran my hand across the top of the flames.

"I feel you. So warm, not boiling hot like momma used to tell me the fire of hell felt like. She's probably burning there now." I then mumbled, *"The bitch."*

The candles flickered stronger.

"Sorry."

I observed a statue of Jesus. It rested on a pedestal behind the candle stand. The stand held several dozen candles nestled inside small red jars. In front of the stand was a prayer kneeler.

Most of the candles had been lit by people. Some still remained dark. I related to both types. I understood the lit candles because of the fire. To me, fire represented the anger I felt burning within and also the light I longed to be bathed in. I valued the unlit candles because of their darkness. They had no light and were unchosen, much like me. I thought it to be a much-deserved punishment for all that I had done in my pathetic life thus far.

When I stared upwards at the statue of Jesus, my legs gave out. I unintentionally yelled, "Jesus!" and reached backward with my right arm and grabbed the back of a pew for support.

I was too high on *dirt*. I had not eaten, nor slept in days. Plus, the emotional rollercoaster ride I had endured since the death of Chloe. It finally caught up to me. I was exhausted.

"Wait a minute", I said, as I regained my composure and stumbled back towards the statue of Jesus and the rows of flickering candles.

"Jesus starts with the letter "J". God! I can't escape that fuc…I mean, dang letter even in a church."

I felt defeated.

"Why? Why? Why?" I shouted out.

The air conditioner responded with a loud click as it shut off until the next cycle.

"Figures."

I tipped my head slightly to the right, and then to the left at the Jesus statue. I had never been inside a church before in my life. I was clueless about how to behave or what to say. I looked upwards at the ceiling and honestly awaited a lightning bolt to strike me dead.

"The nerve of me to be in such a sacred place. I know."

Momma used to say to me, "You are so disgusting to God. If you dared to set foot inside His house, He would strike your sorry ass dead with a bolt of lightning before you even blinked those same eyes you love to bat at my men so much."

"I hope lightning bolts are striking you non-stop wherever you are now, momma! Liar! I came through the doors of this church and not one bolt of lightning hit me."

I remained fixated on the ceiling and waited a little longer for the deadly strike to happen. After two minutes, nothing. It was confirmed. I hissed, "Should've known you were full of crap like always, momma."

My gaze dropped downward. It briefly halted on Jesus' eyes, before it continued down to His feet. Lightning bolts or not, I still felt ashamed to be inside a church.

"I don't belong here. Liar or not, momma's right. I am disgusting."

A red piece of paper taped to the wall caught the corner of my eye. I said, "What the hell is that?" I squinted my eyes hard and tried to read it. I mumbled the words out loud to help better understand them in my wasted condition.

"One. Identify a candle that has not been lit. Two. Select an unlit match from the box of matches sitting near the candles. Three. Using the flame from a lit candle, light the match. Four. Light the unlit candle of your choice. Five. Make a donation for the candle."

I released a sigh. "I can do that."

I chose an unlit candle on the bottom shelf, took a match from the box, put it over a lit candle and the match sparked.

"Holy sh…!" I quickly recalled I was in a church and whispered, *"Sorry."*

I lit the candle, shook the match and put it on a white ceramic plate with the other used matches. I wanted to jump onto the plate so badly and join them. I felt as burned out and used as them.

I re-read the last line on the red paper again. "Make a donation for the candle."

"A donation?" I asked, confused. "What kind of donation do they want? Money? Because if it's that, I don't have any."

I rummaged through my pockets. I had nothing but a powder coated, used bag of *dirt* and Chloe's lone feather.

"Not giving you those."

I shoved the baggie and feather deeper into their respective pockets. I was unsure of what to do. I feared my candle would be extinguished and my cries unheard if I offered nothing.

I threw a nervous glance around the church and searched the floor for loose change. I found nothing.

I said in a note of sarcasm to the statue, "This is different. I'm usually the one who asks for," I used air-quotes, "'donations' before any kneeling."

I felt as if the statue looked down upon me with pity.

"Don't look at me like that. You know it's the truth."

The statute remained silent.

"Look, all I got to donate for the candle is myself. I know I'm not worth shit." I whispered, "*Sorry. I'm trying not to cuss. Force of habit. I mean with the ass…I mean jerks I deal with. Well, you know. I'll try and do better.*"

I released a loud sigh and resumed my original speech. "I know I'm not worth anything. I know I don't deserve to be inside a church. I know I don't deserve to be talking to you. I don't even know if you can hear me. Or, if you want to hear me." I almost started to cry. "I don't know anything anymore. I just hope I'm enough for a candle and…" I then whispered, "*…some of your time.*"

I knelt on the prayer kneeler with a wobble. I was still very high. My eyes stared at Jesus' feet. I clasped my hands together.

I looked up at Jesus, winked and said, "Saw people do this with their hands in a movie once on our television back when I lived in the trailer with momma. By the way, I like your toes."

I felt confused and nervous. I had no idea what to say. In my head, I swore I had heard Chloe talk to me in that moment. She said, "Close your eyes and let your heart speak, Bug."

And so, I did.

I opened my mouth and stammered out, "I-I never prayed before. I – I don't know how to start. I don't even know why I'm here."

I opened my eyes and looked up at Jesus again. Perhaps for his approval, but probably more for his help. I suddenly found myself mesmerized and confused at the same time.

"You know something? You have kind eyes like that priest. He looked at me just like you are. Like I never done nothing bad my whole life. But I know you know that isn't true. I've done lots of bad stuff. Really bad stuff."

I lowered my head as humiliation washed over me, along with various tainted, sour memories.

"I had lots of bad stuff done to me."

I shook my head side to side as I recalled the countless number of men who took advantage of me. Their images seared deep inside my brain. I rustled the back of my filthy blonde hair with my left hand like a dog with an itch. I attempted to toss the bad memories off me like unwanted fleas.

I was so embarrassed about my life. I then worried because Jesus had seen me with all those men since I was five years old up until now.

Momma always said, "God sees everything you do. So, you can't lie to Him and tell Him you ain't no filthy jezebel because you are! He's seen you and the nasty things you've done!"

"I hate you, momma!" I yelled out before anger, fear and abandonment took over.

"I changed my mind. I don't want to talk about the dirty stuff done to me. Or the dirty stuff I have done to myself. I might vomit."

I thought of Chloe.

"I miss Chloe so much. You would've liked her. She loved everyone. I guess. I don't know. The things she wrote in her diary were so different than who she was on the streets. But I know she loved me. I know it. I suppose she was the only one who ever really did. Well, except for momma in the beginning of my life before her boyfriend's got a hold of me."

I wiped a tear from my eye.

"Jesus? Why is Chloe gone and I'm still here? I don't understand."

I sucked loose snot back up into my nose. "I feel like I really fuc…I mean, screwed up with Chloe. I shouldn't have left her alone for so long. I blame myself for what happened. It's all my fault she's dead. I murdered her. I'm going to burn in hell even more now, huh?"

I shook my head side to side, as I fought my inner demons. In an agitated voice I argued out loud with myself. "No! No! No! Bug. Chloe told you it was okay. It was not your fault what happened to her. You tried to warn her. Tiny only. Tiiiinnnnyyyy ooonnnnlllllyyyy! Chloe didn't listen. It's her fault she's dead, not yours. It was her fault not yours. It was her fault not yours. No, it was mine. All mine. All mine. All mine."

I stared up into the Jesus statue's eyes and sought reassurance from Him that it was not my fault Chloe had died. He only offered more pity.

My head dropped down, and I sobbed uncontrollably and blubbered, "I'm so sorry Chloe. I'm so sorry. I'm so sorry. I'm so sorry," I heaved. "I don't know what to do without her. Tell me. Please." I begged.

The Jesus statue remained silent and stoic.

"Thanks for nothing."

I became overwhelmed with emotion and passed out.

Devoted

Light.

Dark.

Light.

Dark.

Light.

A buzzing sound and ceiling lights that flickered awakened me. At first I had thought it to be the priest. Perhaps he saw me and turned the light switch off and on to wake me up. It soon was apparent the lights that flickered above my head were due to a bulb about to die. The kind priest was not there.

I wiped the drool off the side of my face, regained my bearings and started to chat with the Jesus statue again.

"I don't understand why all those men did such disgusting things to me when I was little. Always wanting to make the letter

'J' with me once the alcohol had put momma to sleep. Why did they do it? Why did they hurt me?"

I grew angry.

"I gave up my dream of being a nurse to care for that evil bitch until the day she croaked."

I wagged my index finger at the statue. "Did you know not once did she ever say sorry for what her men had done to me. Not once. Even though I changed her shitty diapers, cleaned up her vomit and put up with her endless hurtful, hateful words."

I slammed my hand down hard on the top of the prayer kneeler.

"Not once did she ever say it wasn't my fault. She always blamed me, instead."

I slammed my hand down hard on the top of the prayer kneeler again for emphasis.

"Not once did she ever believe me when I told her the truth."

I slammed my hand down again.

"Not!"

Another slam.

"Even!"

Again, with a slam.

"Once!"

My anger meshed into sadness again.

"Maybe it really was my fault. Maybe I stole momma's boyfriends like she said. Maybe I deliberately got hooked on *dirt* to forget. Maybe I wanted to become a whore on the streets and not a nurse in a hospital. Maybe I wanted Chloe to die, so I could die now, too. I have nothing to live for anymore. I'm such a piece of shit, aren't I?"

I looked up at Jesus' eyes.

"You don't have to answer that question. I already know I am."

My anger flared back up.

"I hate myself! I hate them! Every one of those fucking men! I can't close my eyes anymore without seeing them mount me one after the other."

I grabbed chunks of my own hair in an attempt to physically yank the disturbed memories out of my head. The rustling of my hair, the shaking of my head had not been enough to complete the job. Those memories held on to my hair strands with all their might and refused to release me. It was a tug-of-war from hell.

"Let…me…go!"

"No!"

"Let….me…goooooo!"

"Nooooo!"

"LET! ME! GO!" I then threw clumps of hair to the floor and felt a momentary glimpse of victory. "Take that you motherfu…perverts!"

Silence fell over the church and inside my mind simultaneously. But the silence did not last for long. The horrible memories soon returned with vengeance.

I looked up at His eyes with my own eyes, they pleaded for help.

"Why won't they leave? No matter what I do to make it all stop. The visions. The voices. The pain. None of it goes away."

I hugged myself.

"I constantly feel their soft hands, their calloused hands, their rough hands, touching me in every wrong place. Whispering nasty things into my small, delicate ears. Begging me to call them 'Daddy'. They're not my daddy. I don't even know who my real daddy is. I'm not sure momma did either. She just assumed it may have been this one guy. If the truth were known, I think momma was the actual whore in our demented family."

I shivered at the thought of the countless repulsive hands and vile, nasty words.

"I feel so vile. Like a legion of demons have squatted inside every crevasse of my body. My soul feels trapped inside a temple riddled with mass destruction. I don't understand why all those men did such disgusting things to me. Why would they want to do those disgusting things to anyone, ever? What did I do to make them want me? Why won't someone tell me the truth?"

I gritted my teeth and hissed, "I can't stand the way I feel about myself anymore. I want it over with. All of it!"

I wiped fallen tears away. "How do I silence the anger and the hatred? How do I erase all of it from my head? Tell me, please?"

I looked up at the statue as the tears continued to pour down my rosy cheeks.

"I'm *sooooo* tired of running from my past, Jesus. I don't have the strength to outrun it anymore. I'm sick of crawling in the *dirt*. It doesn't work anymore. *Dirt's* not there for me like it used to be. My soul is suffocated by so much hate and anger built up inside of me. I need to let go and be free, like petal head. But I'm scared. I'm all alone now. No Chloe. And now, no *dirt*. I have no one. Nothing."

I sniffled.

"I don't know who I am anymore without *dirt*. I don't know who I want to be. I don't know how to start over with so much bad stuff in my life. Please, help me."

I then released a loud sigh. I said nothing for a few moments. I was unequivocally drained by my giant emotional purge. I had finally opened the door to set the pain and hatred free from my heart and without realizing it, allowed Jesus in. I wiped my face free from what tears lingered and placed my hands into my pockets for a tissue. I did not have one.

"Is it okay if I rest here with you for a while? I'm exhausted."

I did not wait for His response. I leaned forward and hugged Jesus at the ankles. As I turned my head to the left to rest my right cheek upon the top of his feet, the right palm of my hand opened up, and the baggie of dirt dropped to the floor behind Him. In my left hand, Chloe's feather remained.

I whispered, "Thank you, Jesus," and closed my eyes.

My Coda

"**V**ictims of dirt are more than society's throwaways. They are someone's daughter, mother, grandmother, aunt, uncle, cousin, son, father, and friend. If you happen upon a firefly soaring over a dewy meadow, look for me….in the light."

If you would like to be healed from past hurts, be able to have forgiveness, be able to make a change in your life and be able to have an honest relationship with God, please see *The Salvation Prayer* below to help open the door to your broken heart so God can begin healing you. This is not about religion. This is about healing and having a relationship with God.

The Holy Bible says:

Jesus said to them: *"I am the way, the truth, and the life. No one can come to the Father except through me."* (John 14:6)

"For whosoever calls upon the name of the Lord shall be saved." (Romans 10:13)

If you would like to receive the gift that God has for you today, pray this with your heart and lips out loud:

"Dear Lord Jesus, come into my heart. Forgive me of my sin. Wash me and cleanse me. Set me free. Thank You that you died for me. I believe that You are risen from the dead and that You are coming back again for me. Fill me with the Holy Spirit. Give me a passion for the lost, a hunger for the things of God and a holy boldness to preach the gospel of Jesus Christ. I am saved; I am born again; I am forgiven, and I am on my way to heaven because I have Jesus in my heart."

All your sins are forgiven. God loves you and has a great plan for your life.

You are going to be okay, kid!

Each year, approximately 4,400 children commit suicide due to bullying. *Bullied Dying to Fit In* is every bullied person's story and needs to be heard. Will you listen? The book captures the raw emotional side of bullying. Though everyone's bully story is different, the pain felt is the same. The broken heart tells the tale. *Bullied Dying to Fit In* takes the bullied, the non-bullied and even the bully on an emotional roller-coaster of tears, insight, and triumph. For Teens, Parents, School Counselors & Teachers.

Bullied: Dying to Fit In was nominated for the Advocacy/ Social Justice Award for the 2019 In the Margins Book Award.

Visit **www.normandydpiccolo.com** for more information.

Why is Kristyn A. Kutter made the TOP 10 FOR 2021 In the Margins Book Award: School Library Journal.

Instead of talking about her problems, Kristyn A. Kutter's rebellious spirit and self-hate has led to episodes of depression and self-mutilation when things go wrong. It did not help that her best friend committed suicide, leaving her to wonder if she will end up the same way. This book arms the reader with resources for crisis intervention through national centers and online support sites.

***Trigger Warning:** Includes strong language, non-graphic depictions of self-harm, drug and alcohol usage and sexual situations. Recommended for ages 16+*.

About Normandy D. Piccolo

Hello. I am Normandy D. Piccolo. I am an award-winning author, book reviewer, advertising copywriter and freelance journalist. I have written several books, appeared on TV Talk Shows and in Mom Blogs, written radio scripts for the "Click It or Ticket" national campaign featuring Charlie Daniels and The Chicks (formally known as the Dixie Chicks). I have also written radio/TV scripts for St. Jude Children's Research Hospital. I was also nominated for a D&AD Award for my work on "Operation Lifesaver".

My song, "My Bestfriend Ted," received continuous airplay on Chicago radio. Additionally, I worked on the GodSpeaks Billboard campaign contributing campaign concepts, along with scripts for the televised cartoon, Auto-B-Good. I am a participant of the Hillsborough County Anti-Bullying Advisory Committee. My latest book, *Bullied: Dying to Fit In* was nominated for the Advocacy / Social Justice Award for the 2019 In the Margins Book Award.

My book *Why is Kristyn A. Kutter?* made the 2021 In the Margins Book Award TOP 10 List for Fiction/Non-Fiction and the Fiction Recommendation List for 2021.

Additional information, including radio, magazine, and TV interviews, can be seen at www.normandydpiccolo.com

Bug
Book Summary

Bug follows the life of Tobi "Bug" Jackson, as she faces cycles of trauma, addiction, and homelessness while seeking redemption, symbolized by fireflies as light amid darkness.

The story explores Bug's abusive past, struggles with drug and loss, her relationships with a free-spirited homeless friend and a compassionate priest, and her journey toward healing after further tragedy.

Bug is a poignant exploration of trauma, addiction, and the possibility of healing, emphasizing compassion for those struggling with addiction.

The author, Normandy D. Piccolo, is an award-winning writer often known for addressing social issues in her work.

9 780997 934991